I0761988

BOOKS BY BLAKE PIERCE

RACHEL GIFT MYSTERY SERIES
HER LAST WISH (Book #1)
HER LAST CHANCE (Book #2)
HER LAST HOPE (Book #3)

AVA GOLD MYSTERY SERIES
CITY OF PREY (Book #1)
CITY OF FEAR (Book #2)
CITY OF BONES (Book #3)

A YEAR IN EUROPE
A MURDER IN PARIS (Book #1)
DEATH IN FLORENCE (Book #2)
VENGEANCE IN VIENNA (Book #3)
A FATALITY IN SPAIN (Book #4)
SCANDAL IN LONDON (Book #5)
AN IMPOSTOR IN DUBLIN (Book #6)
SEDUCTION IN BORDEAUX (Book #7)
JEALOUSY IN SWITZERLAND (Book #8)
A DEBACLE IN PRAGUE (Book #9)

ELLA DARK FBI SUSPENSE THRILLER
GIRL, ALONE (Book #1)
GIRL, TAKEN (Book #2)
GIRL, HUNTED (Book #3)
GIRL, SILENCED (Book #4)
GIRL, VANISHED (Book 5)
GIRL ERASED (Book #6)

LAURA FROST FBI SUSPENSE THRILLER
ALREADY GONE (Book #1)
ALREADY SEEN (Book #2)
ALREADY TRAPPED (Book #3)
ALREADY MISSING (Book #4)

EUROPEAN VOYAGE COZY MYSTERY SERIES
MURDER (AND BAKLAVA) (Book #1)

DEATH (AND APPLE STRUDEL) (Book #2)
CRIME (AND LAGER) (Book #3)
MISFORTUNE (AND GOUDA) (Book #4)
CALAMITY (AND A DANISH) (Book #5)
MAYHEM (AND HERRING) (Book #6)

ADELE SHARP MYSTERY SERIES
LEFT TO DIE (Book #1)
LEFT TO RUN (Book #2)
LEFT TO HIDE (Book #3)
LEFT TO KILL (Book #4)
LEFT TO MURDER (Book #5)
LEFT TO ENVY (Book #6)
LEFT TO LAPSE (Book #7)
LEFT TO VANISH (Book #8)
LEFT TO HUNT (Book #9)
LEFT TO FEAR (Book #10)
LEFT TO PREY (Book #11)
LEFT TO LURE (Book #12)
LEFT TO CRAVE (Book #13)

THE AU PAIR SERIES
ALMOST GONE (Book#1)
ALMOST LOST (Book #2)
ALMOST DEAD (Book #3)

ZOE PRIME MYSTERY SERIES
FACE OF DEATH (Book#1)
FACE OF MURDER (Book #2)
FACE OF FEAR (Book #3)
FACE OF MADNESS (Book #4)
FACE OF FURY (Book #5)
FACE OF DARKNESS (Book #6)

A JESSIE HUNT PSYCHOLOGICAL SUSPENSE SERIES
THE PERFECT WIFE (Book #1)
THE PERFECT BLOCK (Book #2)
THE PERFECT HOUSE (Book #3)
THE PERFECT SMILE (Book #4)
THE PERFECT LIE (Book #5)
THE PERFECT LOOK (Book #6)

THE PERFECT AFFAIR (Book #7)
THE PERFECT ALIBI (Book #8)
THE PERFECT NEIGHBOR (Book #9)
THE PERFECT DISGUISE (Book #10)
THE PERFECT SECRET (Book #11)
THE PERFECT FAÇADE (Book #12)
THE PERFECT IMPRESSION (Book #13)
THE PERFECT DECEIT (Book #14)
THE PERFECT MISTRESS (Book #15)
THE PERFECT IMAGE (Book #16)
THE PERFECT VEIL (Book #17)
THE PERFECT INDISCRETION (Book #18)
THE PERFECT RUMOR (Book #19)

CHLOE FINE PSYCHOLOGICAL SUSPENSE SERIES
NEXT DOOR (Book #1)
A NEIGHBOR'S LIE (Book #2)
CUL DE SAC (Book #3)
SILENT NEIGHBOR (Book #4)
HOMECOMING (Book #5)
TINTED WINDOWS (Book #6)

KATE WISE MYSTERY SERIES
IF SHE KNEW (Book #1)
IF SHE SAW (Book #2)
IF SHE RAN (Book #3)
IF SHE HID (Book #4)
IF SHE FLED (Book #5)
IF SHE FEARED (Book #6)
IF SHE HEARD (Book #7)

THE MAKING OF RILEY PAIGE SERIES
WATCHING (Book #1)
WAITING (Book #2)
LURING (Book #3)
TAKING (Book #4)
STALKING (Book #5)
KILLING (Book #6)

RILEY PAIGE MYSTERY SERIES
ONCE GONE (Book #1)

ONCE TAKEN (Book #2)
ONCE CRAVED (Book #3)
ONCE LURED (Book #4)
ONCE HUNTED (Book #5)
ONCE PINED (Book #6)
ONCE FORSAKEN (Book #7)
ONCE COLD (Book #8)
ONCE STALKED (Book #9)
ONCE LOST (Book #10)
ONCE BURIED (Book #11)
ONCE BOUND (Book #12)
ONCE TRAPPED (Book #13)
ONCE DORMANT (Book #14)
ONCE SHUNNED (Book #15)
ONCE MISSED (Book #16)
ONCE CHOSEN (Book #17)

MACKENZIE WHITE MYSTERY SERIES
BEFORE HE KILLS (Book #1)
BEFORE HE SEES (Book #2)
BEFORE HE COVETS (Book #3)
BEFORE HE TAKES (Book #4)
BEFORE HE NEEDS (Book #5)
BEFORE HE FEELS (Book #6)
BEFORE HE SINS (Book #7)
BEFORE HE HUNTS (Book #8)
BEFORE HE PREYS (Book #9)
BEFORE HE LONGS (Book #10)
BEFORE HE LAPSES (Book #11)
BEFORE HE ENVIES (Book #12)
BEFORE HE STALKS (Book #13)
BEFORE HE HARMS (Book #14)

AVERY BLACK MYSTERY SERIES
CAUSE TO KILL (Book #1)
CAUSE TO RUN (Book #2)
CAUSE TO HIDE (Book #3)
CAUSE TO FEAR (Book #4)
CAUSE TO SAVE (Book #5)
CAUSE TO DREAD (Book #6)

KERI LOCKE MYSTERY SERIES
A TRACE OF DEATH (Book #1)
A TRACE OF MUDER (Book #2)
A TRACE OF VICE (Book #3)
A TRACE OF CRIME (Book #4)
A TRACE OF HOPE (Book #5)

CHAPTER ONE

When Diana St. James was a child, she used to sit on the carpet of her grandmother's living room in Long Island, where she'd listen to Strauss' waltzes and Mozart's symphonies and all other kinds of classical music, lilting from an old-time record player, until she knew every note by heart. Sometimes, her grandfather would pull her up and spin her around the living room, while she stood upon his toes, giggling wildly.

She smiled at the thought as the express train smoothly bulleted toward Vienna, which was finally coming into view over the horizon. The green hills were giving way to small villages, and now the historic buildings of the city were visible, rising above the verdant trees. *If only my grandparents could see me now. Here, in the City of Music!*

She peered out the window at the green, rolling countryside, full of sleepy towns with thatched roofs and residents who happily waved at her, as if they'd never seen a train before. Occasionally, the train would zip through a deep forest so lush she could almost smell the pine trees. The majestic, snow-capped Alps rose in the distance, and she marveled at the sheer size of them. She'd watched *The Sound of Music* a thousand times, but no movie could ever beat the real thing. Julie Andrews was right; the hills *were* alive. It sort of did make her want to run through them, spinning and singing.

Never had she thought she'd actually visit Austria. And Vienna? This was where all of the legends of classical music had flourished, learning the craft and creating their masterpieces.

A little thrill travelled down her spine, and she leaned so close to the window that she nearly pressed her nose against it.

She clutched her itinerary to her chest as she thought about what she'd like to do first when she stepped off the train. Always a planner, when she'd been the Marketing Director at *Addict* cosmetics in New York City, she'd followed her schedule to a T. When she left JFK airport, she'd actually mapped out stops at popular tourist sights down to the hour, only to have the schedule fall apart mere minutes after the plane touched down at Charles de Gaulle. But now, on her third stop on her whirlwind, year-long tour of Europe, her trusty, leather-bound book had changed. After adventures in France and in Italy, she'd come to expect that nothing ever went according to plan.

So now, the book was a bit of a bucket list. It didn't include stops at all the most popular tourist traps. Sure, it would be nice to see those, but instead, she'd filled the book with the things in her heart that she *really* wanted.

So her only plans for Austria were simple ones: *Be moved to tears by beautiful music.*

In a city known for its music, she figured there'd be a lot of opportunity for that.

In fact, she'd taken the train to Vienna on a whim, without putting much thought into where she'd stay or what she'd do once she got here. How crazy. How unlike her. *If only my coworkers at Addict could see me now! They might not even recognize me,* she thought, as she shuffled to the edge of her seat, preparing to disembark.

As she did, an older woman toddled toward the exit, clutching the back of the seat with one hand and a cane with the other. When the slowing train suddenly lurched forward, she stumbled with it. Diana lunged over to steady her, quickly moved her bag from the seat, and guided the woman into it. *"Danke,"* the woman said. She had fiery red hair, streaked with white, and a cherubic, unwrinkled face.

"Are you all right?" Diana asked as the woman, a little stunned, settled into her seat.

"Oh, yes. I'm in a bit of a rush to get off," she said with a pronounced accent. "I'm meeting my grandchildren in Vienna and I don't move as quickly as I used to. I don't want the train pulling away before I've had a chance to drag my body off it!"

"Well, I'll be happy to help you when you the train comes to a stop," Diana said, smiling until her eyes were caught by something out the opposite window. She gasped at the sight of a magnificent old castle, buried high in the mountains, swathed in wisps of fog, like some sort of fantasy story come to life.

"Thank you. Is it your first time in Vienna?"

Diana nodded. "My first time in Austria. In Europe, actually. I'm spending a year here, seeing all the sights. I just came from Verona, Italy."

"Oh, very good, very good."

"Is that where you came from?"

"No, I live in Salzburg, but my family is here in Vienna. We are going to dinner tonight, and I'll be visiting with the grandchildren. What will you be seeing while you are here, may I ask?"

Diana looked out the window. "Well, I'm not sure. I—"

"No doubt you will take in some music at the *Musikverein?"*

Diana's eyes widened in surprise and she opened her itinerary. "Actually, it's funny you say that. The only thing I have on my bucket list is to—"

The woman read her writing. "*Be moved to tears by beautiful music?* Ah, the last time I was here, that happened to me. I heard the most wonderful pianist at the great golden hall!" She patted her chest. "I could feel his notes deep in my soul."

"Really? What was his name?"

"Lukas Huber," she said, pointing at the itinerary with one chubby finger. "You write that down. He is young, but he will be a household name, one day, like *Herr* Mozart. He performs his own compositions, but his work on Mozart's Piano Concerto No. 21 was one of the most gorgeous renderings I'd ever heard. You know it, of course?"

"Oh, of course," she said, the ritornello lilting through her head. "It's one of my very favorites, too. But I'm very partial to his twentieth."

The old woman nodded. "I do not know music as well as you do, but you will love Vienna. You can almost hear the music in the air, when you're here. It seems to travel on the breeze."

She laughed at the thought of that. When she was married, Evan had always liked complete silence. But Diana was the one who needed classical music to be playing in the background at all times. It soothed her, lifted her spirits. Music in the air was certainly better than what she had in Long Island, which was the sound of the highway traffic and police sirens, all the time.

"Tell me . . . Is it possible, do you know, to get tickets to a performance at *Musikverein* last-minute? I grew up watching the New Year's concerts from there on television. I heard that there was some sort of lottery to get seats . . .?"

She nodded. "Unfortunately, it is quite difficult to get a seat. It's old, so a rather small venue. For months and months, they are usually booked up. People make reservations years in advance."

"Oh." Her spirits plummeted.

"But don't fear! There is a possibility you can get a standing seat. Perhaps not at *Musikverein* as most of the tourists and university students go there, but the others, *Volksoper* or *Theater an de Wien.* It is possible."

"Theater . . . you mean, isn't that where Beethoven first performed many of his works?"

"That's right."

She gasped. "I totally forgot that was here! I have to go see it."

"Yes, you must! For a music lover such as yourself, I am sure you will enjoy it . . ."

She laughed. "I know nothing about Vienna, but I do know a bit about classical music. My grandparents were very interested in it. My grandmother was a classical pianist, so she loved all of this. I wish she could see me now. In fact, I wish she could be with me now."

"Ah. Then you are in the right place. I'll wish you luck! Maybe you'll get a seat!"

That would be a dream come true! she thought, writing the names of the theaters down on her itinerary as the train slowed to a stop at Vienna Hauptbahnhof, the main station in the city.

Diana grabbed her own bag and helped the woman up. She carefully escorted her down the aisle, helping her take the steps, one by one. When they reached the ground, the woman beamed at her. "Do you know where you are headed?"

Diana looked around at the modern train station as they walked to the doors. It was a bright, sunny day, and the sunshine slashed down through a diamond-shape window above them. She couldn't wait to see the history, the gothic statues and stately marble facades of the old buildings. At least, most people here spoke English, so that would be helpful. She shrugged. "Not really!"

Suddenly, childish voices shouted in unison, *"Oma!"*

Diana turned to see two children, a girl in braids and knee-socks, and a little boy with a mop of blonde hair, running for the woman. They hugged her and spoke in German as a man and woman came and joined in on the hug.

Diana took a step away as the old woman greeted her family, feeling a pang of homesickness for her own children. Though Lily and Bea were grown with lives and families of their own, and though she and her husband Evan were now divorced, she still missed them.

Funny, since she'd just seen them in Verona. Though it had been a crazy few days, in the end, she had to admit, she'd had fun with them.

The old lady smiled at her. "This young woman was kind enough to help me off the train," she explained to her family, then squeezed Diana's hand affectionately. "Enjoy your time in Vienna! And oh, yes. . ." She leaned in and whispered in a conspiratorial way, "Since you don't know where you're headed, and since you're a music lover, go that way."

Diana followed her pointed finger down the busy street. She could make out a few historic buildings mixed in with the modern ones, and statues of various historic and mythological figures, everywhere. There was so much to look at, she wasn't sure what to see first. Meanwhile, travelers from all over flanked them on the wide sidewalk. "That way?"

"Yes. I think you will like what you stumble upon." She winked.

"All right. Thank you!" Diana said as the family walked away, leaving her alone in the shadow of the station.

She shivered. It was definitely colder here than it had been in Verona. Her overbearing ex, Evan, had shown up in the middle of her Italy trip with his far-too-young fiancé, and it had thrown her ideas of exploring Italy alone into a tailspin. It had wound up fine, especially when her daughters Lily and Bea had joined them, but their appearance had kind of thrown a wrench into her trip's purpose, which was for some much-needed, soul-searching alone time.

Now, she was truly alone. There was no one around to rely on, in case something went wrong.

That's fine. That's what you want. What you need!

Her phone dinged. She looked down to see a text from Bea, her newly-engaged youngest daughter, who was living in Japan: *Are you all right?*

Was she? Could she do this herself? Without the help of her family? Part of her thought that was why they'd showed up in Italy, unannounced—because they doubted she could handle vacationing on her own. Evan, once, seemed to think she couldn't, because she'd needed to plan everything so carefully.

But she'd shown him. She'd made it through the adventure in Verona without his help.

And she could do it again. She typed in: *Perfect! Just arrived in Vienna!*

Yes, she could do this, relying only on herself and her own intellect and resourcefulness to make this the trip of her dreams. She tucked her phone away, determined not to rely on it, either. Now, she took a deep breath of crisp air and smiled as she looked down the street, at the direction the old woman had pointed in. A fellow-music-lover had said, *I think you will like what you stumble upon.*

And she couldn't wait to find out what it was, and what new adventure she'd find in the City of Music.

CHAPTER TWO

Diana plucked a tourist map from a display on a street corner, unfolded it, and stared at it.

That lady said I'd like what I found here. But I haven't found very much. I'm not sure what I'm looking for!

She stopped in front of *Karlskirche* a magnificent Baroque cathedral with a blue dome, taking various pictures, and even a selfie, which she promptly sent to Lily to assure her that she hadn't fallen victim to an ax murderer. Her constantly worrying eldest daughter was very worried about ax murderers, for some reason, above all the other dangers that existed out in the wide world.

Walking around the reflecting pond at the front of the building, she read from the map: *The most outstanding Baroque church in Vienna, as well as one of the city's greatest buildings, the church is dedicated to Saint Charles Borromeo, one of the great counter-reformers of the sixteenth century.* She gawked at the sheer size and magnificent statues of angels holding up massive, intricately engraved columns, and the golden eagles perched around the sky-colored domes.

But now, as she looked around, she felt a bit disappointed.

Wow, Diana. You are not easily impressed. One of the most gorgeous pieces of architecture in the world and you can't even summon excitement? Snap out of it.

For some reason, though, she couldn't. It wasn't just a mood. It was about fulfilling a dream. The reason she'd come to Europe in the first place.

Just another touristy sight. Lovely, but I already determined that's not what I came to Europe for. Sure, I want to see these places. But I want more.

She'd read somewhere, something about that. That travel, while meant to broaden one's mind, often had the opposite effect. Instead of a well-travelled person being so thrilled by the many sights in the world, often, they became blasé about their wonder and beauty. The more you see, the harder you are to impress.

Had she become jaded like that, after only three European cities?

No, Diana. It's because you haven't yet seen what is in your heart. Architecture is pretty, but it was never your thing. Italy was the same. The scenery and architecture were lovely, but until you saw that play in Verona, you weren't in love with it, either. Once you hear that beautiful music, you will love Vienna, and truly find what you were looking for on this trip.

She shuffled to set aside the map and pull out her itinerary. *Lukas Huber.* That was his name. She looked up and down the street.

Really, were you thinking that old lady was going to point you in the direction of him?

Well, yes. She actually had *hoped* it would be that easy to find what she was looking for.

Right now, though, she was utterly bewildered.

She should have known. So far, nothing in this trip had come easy. Everything she started out looking for wound up changing to something else entirely. Something completely unexpected, that she never realized she'd wanted.

Something even *better.*

So don't worry about it! Let the road take you where it may.

Right now, the road seemed to be taking her toward what looked like the public toilets.

I suppose I should be looking for a hotel somewhere around here. I should have asked that lady if she knew of any place to stay.

Following the map, she passed the Vienna Institute of Technology, its many stately buildings towering above her, and walked along the sidewalk, almost careening head-first into a few people walking the opposite direction. It wasn't like in New York, though. Most people simply smiled and said, "*Tschuldigung,*" which, from the way they said it, with a smile and without any malice whatsoever, she gathered to mean *Pardon me.* It was refreshing; most people in New York would've at the very least yelled at her to watch where she was going. In some sections of the city, she'd have been lucky to escape with her life.

She walked a little farther, until she noticed an older building with billboards on the wall, advertising what looked like an upcoming show. *Chicago.*

She laughed to herself. *I didn't come all the way from the United States to see Chicago, but that might be interesting . . .*

Diana walked to the front of the building and paused, then looked back at the map. Her eyes widened when she saw the sign above the door.

Theater an der Wien.

She gasped. This was it. The place where Beethoven had debuted some of his most famous compositions. In her head, she played his Piano Concerto No. 4, which had been her grandmother's favorite. Her legs wobbled as she walked closer, to a sign engraved in the wall, underneath bunting with the Austrian flag's bright white and red.

She noticed the word Beethoven, but couldn't read the rest. It was in German.

She squinted for a moment, then stopped a fashionable young woman with a blonde ponytail who was passing by with her pint-sized poodle strutting ahead of her on a leash. "Um, excuse me," she asked, pointing at the sign. "Could you tell me what that says?"

The woman smiled and nodded, then read: "Ludwig van Beethoven lived in the Theater an der Wien in 1803 and 1804. Parts of his opera, the Third Symphony, and the Kreutzer Sonata were written here. *Fidelio* and other works received their first performance in this house."

"Oooh," Diana breathed. "I can't believe I'm actually standing here!"

The woman laughed before walking away, calling, "Music lover, eh? Enjoy!"

Diana stepped forward and couldn't help herself. She touched the rough exterior of the building reverently, slowly stroking her finger over the stone. *Beethoven lived here.*

Then she walked around, marveling at the building with bright yellow walls and green doors. She looked up at the *Papagenotor,* the Papageno Gate, over the former main entry. It was adorned with sandstone sculptures, including that of Papageno, cloaked in feathers, and the child sprites from Mozart's famous opera, *The Magic Flute*. That was another one of her grandparents' favorites. Beyond that was a golden coat of arms. In her head, she couldn't help singing "Papageno, Papagena," just as the characters did in the opera, *Pa pa pa pa . . .*

Then she looked across the street at the sign on the stately brick building across the way. *The Hotel Beethoven.*

She smiled. *Well, I know where I'm staying.*

It was perfect serendipity, she found herself laughing. Is this what the old lady had meant? If so, she had definitely pointed Diana in the right direction. Deciding to push her luck even further, Diana went around to the new main entrance, off the main street, and found her way to the *Theater an der Wien* box office.

"*Guten Tag,*" the mustached man behind the window said.

"Hello," she replied. "I'm wondering if you have any tickets for a performance tonight, or maybe tomorrow?"

"A performance?" His eyes danced with amusement. "*Ja.* What are you looking for? We have plenty of seats for *Chicago.*"

"Oh, no. Not a musical. Classical music. Any kind. I'm a big fan. Do you have any standing room, maybe?"

He chuckled. "Well, you have come to the right city, if you like classical music. But I'm sorry to tell you that most nights are reserved for *Chicago.* We only have one classical performance a week, and you just missed our last one. Our next isn't for six days."

"Oh, no, really?" her spirits plummeted.

"However," he said, "There is a special summer evening concert being performed at *Musikverein* tonight."

"At the *Musikverein?*" she asked in shock.

He nodded, amused by her expression.

"I'm sorry. I was just told it'd be nearly impossible to get a ticket for a performance there."

"Oh, it is. But there are cancellations all the time, so anything's possible!"

"Who is performing?"

He looked down at a brochure, then passed it over to her. "Lukas Huber and the Vienna Philharmonic will be playing Beethoven's Piano Concerto No. Four, among other pieces. I believe he's to debut his newest symphony there, The Jupiter Symphony. It's supposed to be splendid."

Diana just stared at him for a moment, speechless. She had to have been dreaming. Lukas Huber? *Musikverein*? Beethoven's Piano Concerto No. Four? Could there be anything more serendipitous?

When she didn't say anything, he continued, "I can call over to the other hall and see if I can find you a ticket, if you'd like?"

She bobbed her head up and down eagerly. "Oh! Yes! That would be amazing!"

"Just one?"

She nodded. "Yep. It's just me."

"That makes it easier. Standing room, of course. One moment." He disappeared inside the ticket booth for a while, and meanwhile, Diana drummed her fingers on the ledge. As she did, she launched into a fantasy, her, sitting in the front row of the small music hall, surrounded by the spectacularly gilded halls and warm light, listening to the beautiful music as tears streamed down her face.

She was so wrapped up in the fantasy that she barely noticed the man's return until he cleared his throat.

"I apologize. That particular concert is all sold out. Even standing room."

She sighed, defeated. That wasn't how serendipity was supposed to work! How unfair was it to present the perfect option to her, something she'd have travelled the world for, only to snatch it away when she was this close? "Are you sure? Is there another performance, maybe tomo—"

He was already shaking his head. "I'm sorry. It's a one-night engagement." He sniffled. "I'm sorry. Apparently this concert has been sold out for a long time. The man on the phone told me that you have a better chance of getting an invitation to dinner with the Queen of England."

"It's completely sold out? There's not even a single seat?"

He nodded. "Seat? Oh, no. An actual *seat* in that particular venue is even *rarer* than an invitation to dinner with the Queen. Many of those seats are legacy tickets, passed down from generation to generation. Or they're available as a subscription, to the entire season. And single seats are often taken by the performers themselves, for guests. So my only option, really, was to get you a standing room ticket, in the back, which are usually reserved for students from the university and tourists. But, unfortunately, they are all gone."

"Oh. Well. Thank you." For a moment, she thought about asking of other concerts, but she felt so sour about missing that one, the perfect opportunity, that everything else just seemed to pale in comparison.

"There are other concerts, especially outdoor ones, throughout the city. You should check with the university," he said to her encouragingly, noticing her disappointment. "But if you have your heart set on that one, give me your name and phone number. If a ticket comes up, I will call you."

"Would you?" She quickly took the paper he'd offered to her and scribbled her information. "I'm not sure where I'm staying. Probably that hotel across the street. But this is my cell. Call me whenever. I'll be there!"

He laughed. "Well, who knows. Stranger things have happened. It's just one ticket. And university students are notoriously fickle, so one may come available. It's possible. I'll let you know."

She crossed both fingers and smiled. *Please. Please. Please let there be a ticket tonight for me!*

CHAPTER THREE

Could something please go right for me? Diana begged the universe as she crossed the street. *After the perfect-concert-ticket debacle, I don't know how much more I can take.*

She was so upset by the blow that she couldn't help feeling a little negative about Vienna. Like all of her hopes and dreams for the place had been crushed. She approached the front desk of the small but opulent hotel with no reservations in the computer, and yet *plenty* of them in her head. *If they tell me this place is all booked up, I might as well take the train somewhere else.*

"Hello," she said, a little reluctantly.

The woman at the desk smiled at her. "*Guten tag.* Checking in?"

She nodded. "I hope to. I don't have a reservation, though."

The clerk tapped something into her computer. "No problem. We have a room available. How long will you need it for?"

She sighed with relief. "Thank you! Three days, to start?"

"Perfect." She continued to tap on her computer, as Diana handed over her credit card.

The clerk ran it and passed her a key. "We're happy to have you staying with us, Ms. St. James. I have you in a suite at the top floor of the hotel. I'm sure you'll be comfortable but if there's anything you need, please let us know." She pointed to the bank of elevators, behind Diana. "Right that way. Do you need help with your luggage?"

Diana smiled and shook her head, then lifted up the key. "Thank you. No. I'm great."

As she headed into the elevator, she felt like her luck was starting to change. When she opened the door to her room at the Hotel Beethoven suite, she *knew* it. The room was vast, clean, and had the perfect view of Beethoven's theater. She spent a half hour, on the balcony, taking pictures of it, imagining what it had been like in Beethoven's time, when he lived there. As she was snapping photographs, her phone buzzed with a text from Lily: *That's nice. Are you okay?*

She sighed. What was her family thinking? Didn't they trust her at all to be fine, alone in a foreign country? Hadn't her time with them in Italy taught them anything?

Okay, yes. She had almost gotten arrested for murder. But then she and Bea had scoured the city of Verona and found the real killer. No problems. She'd held her own, and everything was fine.

But yes, she had to admit, she had a knack for getting herself in trouble.

Getting herself *out* of it, too. Not that she could tell them *that.*

Besides, as irritating as it could be, she had to remind herself that it was nice to have some people who cared about her, even while she was half a world away.

She typed in: *Yes! Going out to sightsee now! Turning off my phone! So don't worry about me!*

She could just imagine Lily, the more cautious of her daughters, gritting her teeth at that. "Lily" and "Worry" were synonymous. Lily lived and died by her phone, and by careful planning, just like Diana once had. Diana had created a monster in her oldest daughter, one who usually came up with worst-case-scenarios for every possible situation. Thus, the ax-murderer thing.

Diana didn't turn off her phone, though—she'd wanted to use it to take photos—but it had the desired effect. Lily didn't text her back. So she managed to freshen up, change out of her travel clothing and into a fresh pair of shorts and blouse, and equip herself for a fun, sightseeing extravaganza. She hoped that keeping busy would take her mind off the event at *Musikverein* that she was going to miss.

As she went downstairs to the lobby, studying the map, she decided to set out and follow the path of another one of her favorite composers—Johann Strauss, Jr.

She stopped at the concierge, where a small, stout bald man was smiling solicitously at her, eager to help. "Strauss?"

He laughed with a giddy kind of glee. "This town is all about Johann Strauss! What would you like to see?"

She shrugged. "I guess . . . what would you recommend? Let's start with the most famous."

He nodded, took her map, and circled a few things for her, as well as the route to take her there, marking them with stars so she couldn't get lost. "A nice place to get some good photos, since it's a lovely park on a lovely day! You will like it, I am sure."

"Perfect! Thank you," she said, heading off.

As she walked, she saw why the man had laughed. There were quite a lot of attractions in the city dedicated to the famous waltz composer—streets, bookstores, even a pretzel stand on the sidewalk were named after him. The one attraction the concierge recommended she visit on such a lovely day was at the *Stahtpark*—a golden memorial to the composer surrounded by lush greenery and park-like atmosphere.

As she went through the gates of the park, following the map, she noticed an abundance of tourists, all enjoying the weather and the beauty of the place. The stone paths wound through the idyllic greenery, past memorials for other composers, like Franz Lehár, Anton Bruckner, and Franz Schubert. At each one, she snapped a photograph, even though each one was a reminder of the beautiful music she *wouldn't* be able to hear tonight.

She walked past a small river, where ducks floated by lazily, hoping that wasn't the mighty Danube, and crossed a bridge to a lovely, Renaissance era building and gazebo that looked like an outdoor concert venue. Unfortunately, there was no music being played at that moment.

She paused, listening to the wind blowing, and the sound of children playing on the bank of the river, hoping that what the old lady on the train had said was true. No. There was no music in the air at all. Or maybe she was just in such a negative mood that she couldn't hear it.

Sighing, she snapped a few more photos, and then came to a busy section where stood the golden statue of Johann Strauss, Jr., playing a violin. It glistened in the bright sun, so blindingly that she had to raise her hand to shield her eyes from the sight. There was a long line of tourists, waiting to snap a picture with the King of the Waltz.

Well, if I can't listen to his music, at least I can get a picture of him.

Diana got on the line, still studying the map. After this, she'd go to Strauss' birthplace. His grave. Oh, and there was a museum nearby that could be interesting.

It was all very lovely.

But it wasn't soulful, emotional *music*.

As she followed the line, she noticed a number of men, dressed in period-style outfits, with powdered wigs, waistcoats and knee breeches, waving papers in their hands. Occasionally, they approached people in the line, and while often they were motioned away, sometimes, it appeared that money was exchanged. *What are they selling?* she wondered.

Just as curiosity got the better of her, a man approached and handed her a brochure. It said on the top: *Musikverein.*

Her heart sped up. She tried to read the rest, but it was in German.

"What is this for?"

The man was wearing a terrible, windblown gray wig and white cravat, and his face was powdered a sickly white. She supposed he was dressed up to look like Beethoven. He grinned. "Pretty American! You like music? I can tell you are a woman of distinction, of course you do. You want to see it at the best music hall in all the world?"

She nodded eagerly. It was as if he'd read her mind.

He grinned, showing crooked, yellowing teeth. "We can make it happen."

"You can?" she asked, suspicion creeping in. There were plenty of ticket scalpers all over New York City, and she was wise to them. They were thieves, and she knew it. She'd never be caught dead talking to them. Somehow, she'd thought Austria's people were better than that.

Still . . . if they could get her into *Musikverein* . . .

"I can," he said with a sly wink, reaching for her hand. She snatched it away, slightly disgusted.

Ugh. What am I doing? What a slimeball. So scalpers are all the same, no matter what side of the ocean you're on.

"I'm sorry, but I'm not intere—"

He pulled out a couple of tickets and held them up to her. "Are you sure? You don't want to see the concert at *Musikverein?* It's tonight! A once-in-a-lifetime performance, with Lukas Huber and the Vienna Philharmonic!"

She stared at them. So badly did she want to see the concert that her palms grew slick and she felt her mouth go wet. Her mouth spoke even before her mind had fully weighed the pros and cons. "How much?"

"For you, pretty American?" He grinned wide, revealing a missing eye tooth. "Just four-hundred euros."

She had a bit of an idea what that amounted to, in US dollars—about $500. And maybe she didn't care. Suddenly, spending far too much money on a ticket for a concert that she *really* wanted to see didn't sound like such a bad idea. "And that's for one ticket?"

"Yes. That's right."

She was probably being taken advantage of. No, scratch that. She *knew* she was definitely being taken advantage of. The ticket looked legit, but he was probably making a huge profit on it. She hesitated.

The man looked nervously around, clearly anxious to close the deal. "It's something you'll never see again in all your life. If this is your vacation, make it memorable! You only live once, right? Imagine, being there, at the debut of Beethoven's greatest symphonies, symphonies that have been played the world over, millions and millions of times. But you get to hear it first. History is going to be made on that stage tonight," he whispered, leaning in. "They say Lukas Huber is the next great composer of our lifetime. His *Liebeskonzert* was so well-received when it was performed her last month that it stunned the world. He'll be debuting his next creation tonight. Early word is, The Jupiter Symphony*?* It is a masterpiece. That is why this performance has been sold out for most of the year."

Sold.

She reached for her purse, sliding open the zipper. Taking out her wallet, she carefully looked around to make sure no one was watching her as she opened it. "Well, I—"

"Move along, *der Gauner,"* a thick man with a red mustache and almost equally red face said, shaking a fist at them. "You're nothing but a crook! Bilking these tourists out of their money! For shame!"

"But—" Diana said as the two men in period costumes scattered away like cockroaches in a kitchen light. Clearly, they were frightened by this refrigerator-sized man.

"No need to thank me," the man said with a smile. He was wearing shorts that seemed to go up almost to his breastbone and had no discernable waist whatsoever. Also, white sports socks to the knees, and a Tyrolean hat, tilted at a jaunty angle. "Those pests are always out here, disturbing me while I try to enjoy my afternoon stroll."

She sighed. "I really wanted to see that concert, though. So I—"

"Ah. But those crooks charge you four-hundred euros? For a ticket that costs no more than eighty? That's robbery! It's a shame. You can do better."

"But I—"

He thrust a hand out to her. "Hans."

His hands were like giant paws. She stared at it before shaking it lightly. And she thought *she* was sweating, in the heat. His hand was even sweatier and more unpleasant than hers was. "Diana."

"It's really no trouble. I hate to see tourists of our fair city taken advantage of. We Austrians are not thieves. You're American, eh?"

Diana nodded. "Yes. I'm from New York, so I know a little bit about scalping, and I was actually—"

"There are plenty of places in town to hear good music. You don't have to go to the tourist halls."

She sighed. "I guess you're right. I guess I don't need to see the concert that badly," she said, though she wasn't sure. The man was clearly a snake oil salesman, but he'd made that concert sound so good. What if Huber was the next Mozart? The lady on the train had seemed to think so. What if he was debuting the greatest piece of music the world had ever known, and she could be in the concert hall where it was born? What a story she could tell her grandchildren!

"Well, enjoy your tour, maybe I'll see you around," he said with a broad smile, strolling away as she scanned the area for the scalpers. Maybe, when she got off the line, she could find them, before they sold the tickets to someone else. She *really* wanted to see the concert. Suddenly, four-hundred euros felt almost inconsequential.

But the two men were nowhere in sight. She craned her neck, trying to find them, but they'd disappeared among the greenery.

Then she looked anxiously at the line. It was dragging. A bunch of teenagers were near it, taking selfie after selfie and giggling. At this rate, she'd never get a photo with Strauss' statue.

Forget it. Letting out a grunt of frustration, she stepped out of her place in the line, hoisted her bag higher onto her shoulder, and headed past a line of trees, in search of the ticket scalpers. *I need that ticket!*

She broke into a bit of a run as she scanned the area, looking for the men. But she couldn't see them anywhere. She crossed the bridge over the "Danube," then stood on her tip-toes, trying to find the men among the many hedges and park visitors.

They were gone.

"Ugh!" she growled, dragging a hand down her face. If only Hans hadn't come by. She'd be skipping off to her hotel right now, getting ready for the night of a lifetime. *A once in a lifetime experience.*

Just then, her phone buzzed. She stared at the display, hoping it was notification from the box office that some miracle had come through. But it was a text from Evan: *Hi Love. Back in the states. Where are you?*

She sighed and typed in: *The Music City.*

If only she could get a chance to *witness* some of that music!

A moment later, the response came back: *? What happened? Lily said you were in Austria? How did you get to Nashville? Are you okay?*

She wanted to toss her phone into the trickling little "Danube." Her ex-husband was a brilliant surgeon, but he'd never been much of a world traveler. Once, she'd met Yo Yo Ma, the famous cellist, in New York City, which had to have been her most thrilling celebrity encounter ever. When she came home and told him, he'd looked at her, and quite seriously, said, "You bought a yo yo?"

No, I am not okay! I am totally annoyed! And you're only contributing to it!

She wanted to type that, but she restrained herself. Instead, she typed in: *Evan, no. I am within walking distance of the greatest music hall in the entire world.*

His response: *So you're in New York?*

She clutched her phone in a death grip and rolled her eyes to the heavens. Contrary to what Evan believed, Carnegie Hall wasn't the only music venue in the free world. Far from it.

Before she could respond with something that was destined to be snarky, considering how riled-up she was, her phone actually started to ring, with a foreign number.

She answered. "Yes?"

"Hello. Is this Diana St. James?" The voice was female, but unfamiliar.

"Yes?"

"This is Leonie Winkler. I called the ticket office and heard that you might be interested in a ticket to tonight's performance. I have one that we will not be using, and I wondered if you'd be interested in purchasing it from me?"

Diana's heart jumped in her chest. She gripped the phone tightly, half-wondering if she was hearing things. "Are you sure? You don't want it?"

"Quite sure. I can't use it, actually. Something came up, you see."

"Oh. Yes! Yes! I'd love to," she gushed, speaking so fast her words tumbled out atop one another. "Just name the time and place, and I'll be there!"

"Meet me at the café in the lobby of the Strauss Hotel, in twenty minutes?"

“Yes!” She said, already rushing for the park’s exit in search of a taxi. “Thank you so much!”

CHAPTER FOUR

By now, it seemed to Diana like every place in town was named after some famous composer or another, and the place where Diana arranged to meet Leonie Winkler was no exception. It was called Café Johann Strauss, in the lobby of a modern hotel, not far from her own hotel. Where Diana thought it might contain décor with pieces of his music, old instruments, and the like, there was nothing of the sort, here—it contained bare walls and minimal décor, as seemed to be the style of much of the newer parts of the city.

The cafe was practically empty at that time of day, right before the dinner rush, so when she stepped inside and instantly locked eyes with a young, pretty woman with flowing dark hair and a red silken neck scarf, she smiled.

"Diana?" The woman said as she approached her booth.

"Leonie?" She asked, motioning to the seat across from her.

She nodded and pointed to her carafe. "Please sit. Be my guest. Coffee?"

Diana slipped in and shook her head. "Thank you so much for getting in touch. I was so excited when I heard about the performance, but it broke my heart to learn that it was sold out—" she stopped when she noticed the woman's gorgeous pendant, beneath her red scarf. "Goodness, that's lovely!"

The woman touched the round disk pendant, holding it up to the light so Diana could see the amber and gray stripes through it. "Thank you."

"Anyway, Beethoven's 4th Piano Concerto is one of my favorite pieces of music, and I've always dreamed of seeing a performance there."

The woman nodded. "Of course, it's been sold out for ages. Lukas Huber is a true genius." She touched her heart. "I've been a fan of his for many years. Have you ever seen him perform?"

As Diana shook her head, her phone buzzed in her hand. It was a text from Bea. *Mommy? Wait . . . Dad said you went to Nashville? Please text back. I'm worried about you.*

"No. I haven't." She sighed and typed in: *No. I'm in Vienna.*

Diana looked up, suddenly remembering she was in the midst of a conversation. "I'm sorry. No. Kid problems. But you are not the first to tell me that Lukas Huber is a great talent, one of the modern masters. It seems like ever since I arrived in Austria this morning, everyone can't get enough of him. He has quite the line of admirers."

She frowned. "Yes. It's true. He is a genius. Not to mention that he's very handsome and has great stage presence. The fans line up at the stage door whenever he performs, crowds upon crowds of them. I'm devastated I won't be able to make it, but I wasn't able to get a sitter for my little one, unfortunately."

A moment later, Diana's phone buzzed again: *Oh. So . . . question. Hai wants to set the wedding for next June in Japan. You won't still be traipsing around Europe then, will you?*

That was odd. Her youngest, Bea, was a free spirit. Diana thought for sure she'd tie the knot while skydiving, or trekking in some jungle, or doing something equally crazy. One never could quite tell with Beatrice St. James. A June wedding in the place where they lived sounded so . . . normal. Maybe that was Hai's influence. Diana hadn't met her future son-in-law yet, but he seemed very mature, very grounded. Perhaps they balanced each other out. Of course, Bea was head over heels for him.

Diana pocketed her phone and came back to the conversation at hand. She was being rude, because of her family constantly bothering her. She needed to stop that.

"I'm sorry, again. Family troubles."

The woman smiled thinly. "Of course, I understand all about family."

"Oh, so you said you have children?" Diana asked, smiling. *And she looks so put-together. I wish I could've said the same for myself when I was that age. I used to go to work with Cheerios in my hair.*

In fact, even now, I have issues with dealing with my family . . . clearly.

"Yes. Just one. She's young; I can't leave her alone," Leonie said shortly, so shortly, it surprised Diana. Usually, people loved to speak on their kids.

"Oh! A daughter? I have two. Daughters make this life an adventure. Of course, Mine are grown now, but they're still providing color to my life." She pointed to her phone. "That was my youngest.

Seems like she can't do a thing without consulting me, even now. She just got engaged last week so she's in a bit of a frenzy, with all the plans!"

The woman didn't comment. She didn't even smile. Instead, she reached for her purse. As she did, Diana noticed a large ring on her ring finger. Diamond. *Maybe she's just intensely private,* Diana thought. *But whoever she's married to is clearly making good money.*

"Anyway, I'm sure you'll appreciate Huber's genius when you see him tonight. You can really get lost in his music. They say he's the next Beethoven, believe it or not, and I believe it. I believe one day his name will be in papers all over the world. That is why the show has been sold out since last year."

Diana shook her head as she gazed at the ticket. It might as well have been a brick of pure gold. "Are you sure you can't find a sitter?" she asked, though the desperately wanted to lunge across the table and take it in her hands. "It seems like such a shame that you—"

"I am," she said, rather curtly. "I'm not out to make any money on the sale of this ticket, so . . . shall we say face value? Eighty euros?"

Diana's eyebrows went up. "Are you sure? I'm more than happy to compensate you for coming all the way--"

The woman shook her head. "No, it's quite all right. I come here often. It was no trouble."

To think, Diana had almost paid nearly five times that to the scalper in the park. Maybe Hans was an angel in disguise.

"That's incredibly generous. I can't believe I have a ticket to it. I heard it was rarer than an invitation to dinner with the Queen of England."

The woman shrugged. "Perhaps. Like I said, he's very good."

"I do feel like I owe you something. Let me at least pay for your coffee."

"No need," the woman said, waving her hands. "It's my pleasure. I'm happy to grant the opportunity to a fervent music lover such as yourself. You will be moved."

"You think so?" Diana asked, opening up her wallet and pulling out the bills. She counted them carefully and slid them across to her. "It's funny that you say that. Because when I was deciding on coming here, my top bucket list item was to be moved to tears by beautiful music."

"Ah. Well, I am sure Lukas Huber will do that for you. Her moves me to tears, just thinking of him." She stared into her coffee for a moment and sighed. "He's truly an artist."

She lifted her coffee with long, slender fingers. Diana couldn't help but stare at the massive diamond ring on her finger as she brought the coffee to her lips, leaving a red imprint on the cup that matched the scarf around her neck.

A woman like her . . . she is well taken care of, I'm sure. She must have a live-in nanny. I can't believe she couldn't get a sitter for tonight! Diana thought, but then shook it away as the woman handed her the ticket. She read the words, again and again, getting lost in them. *Doesn't matter. Whatever happened, it's my gain. I'm going to see Lukas Huber and the Vienna Philharmonic tonight at Musikverein!*

She thanked Leonie Winkler and checked her phone. No more messages from her family, but it was getting late. She rushed from the café, her heart pounding. It was time to get ready for the night of her dreams.

*

Back at her suite in the Hotel Beethoven, Diana slipped into her one nice dress, the one she'd gotten in Verona, put on her heels, and stared at herself in the mirror as she applied a mauve-colored lip gloss. Yes, this would do nicely. *Not too shabby, Mrs. St. James. You look like you belong among the hoity toity types at Musikverein.*

The only thing that would make her fit in more would be a tuxedo-clad man, on her arm.

Stop it, Diana. You were just talking about how this trip was about soul-searching and rediscovering your independence. You don't need anyone else.

She went through the magazine that had been left in the hotel room and found a restaurant right next door to *Musikverein*, called, Restaurant Ludwig, which sounded right up her alley. Calling down to the concierge, she said, "Could you please make me a reservation for one at the Restaurant Ludwig for six o'clock?"

The man cleared his throat. "For one?" he asked, as if he hadn't heard her correctly, or as if she'd made a mistake.

"Yes. That's right. Just one."

It was always the same way. No one seemed to believe that she'd be alone. It was as if they thought she'd made some grave mistake. *Interestingly enough, I can count that high. And I'm sure. It's just me.*

She added, "I'd be fine with bar seating, if they can't accom—"

"One moment."

Likely, everyone who went to these things went as part of a couple. Or they went with family. Never as a single. She'd be alone at the restaurant, unable to engage in any conversation, staring at nothing and trying to avoid the gazes of pity other patrons gave her. And it would probably look odd, getting a glass of wine at intermission, by herself.

But she'd gone on this trip expressly to *be* alone. Because there was something gratifying about self-reliance. It was her way of declaring her independence from her ex-husband, and in doing so, she planned to do just the things that *she* wanted.

Okay, so the impetus for the trip had been a man named Stephane, her old French college boyfriend who'd once wanted to whisk her off to Versailles. She'd missed the chance at that, and had instead wound up meeting Evan. On a silly whim, she'd had the idea that she might arrive at Versailles and pick up with Stephane at their masked ball, as if thirty years hadn't passed in the interim.

Of course, he *hadn't* been there. Instead, she'd had a little adventure with a fake French aristocrat who turned out to be a thief. And she'd met a kind Irishman named Sean. They'd chatted a little, and there had been a few sparks, and he'd said maybe he'd see her again.

But that was the extent of her interaction with him. He'd been the one good man she'd met during her time in Europe. Grabbing her purse, she pulled out the old Gaelic coin he'd given her, when they parted. *Maybe I should text him and see where he is now? He said he might be going to Austria . . .*

Flip a coin. That's what Sean had said to do.

So she flipped it and placed it on the back of her hand. "Heads I text him. Tails, I don't."

She looked at it. Tails.

Hmmm. Fate seems to want me to be alone. But . . . best two out of three?

She swallowed as she thought of Marco, the last man she'd met, in Verona. He'd been an actor, and at the moment she'd seen him, she'd been starstruck. But then he'd been murdered. He'd drank poisoned wine right in front of her, and she'd been a suspect. After a while, it came out that he was a big ladies' man, the kind who invited women backstage all the time.

So no . . . she was pretty much over men. And Sean, as nice as he was, might disappoint her, eventually. *Much* better to be alone.

"*Frau* St. James, your reservation is confirmed," the voice on the phone said. "Table for one at six o'clock sharp. Enjoy your night."

"Thank you."

Just as she hung up the hotel phone, her cell phone buzzed. A message from Lily: *I think I lost my phone charging cable in Verona—it didn't get mixed up with your things, did it?*

Diana groaned.

She typed in *No, sorry,* just as her phone began to ring with a call from Bea. She answered it. "Hello, Bea. And how are you?"

Her daughter sighed dramatically. That was Bea—always the overly dramatic one. "Mommy. I texted you *hours* ago. And you never responded."

"I did! I thought I did."

"Not to my last one. The one about the wedding."

She suddenly remembered the text about the wedding. Something about Hai, and the location, and the date? She really couldn't recall anything else. Her mind was elsewhere, now.

"Sorry! I've been busy. Yes, I'm in Austria, and you'll never believe. I'm going to see a performance at *Musikverein*!"

Instead of the squeals of excitement she anticipated, her youngest said, "Huh? I don't even know what that is."

"It's like a better, more historic version of Carnegie Hall. It's only one of the greatest—"

"Mom. I don't have time to chat. I'm here with Hai and his parents. We're really trying to square away a date for the wedding. So . . . next June?"

Diana fluffed her hair in the mirror. She didn't quite understand how all this needed to be decided right away, considering the date was almost a year in the future. "Well, I don't have a crystal ball so I don't know what will be happening by June, but I'm assuming it's okay."

"You're going to come, aren't you?"

"Of course! What kind of mother do you think I am? Why would you even ask that? I wouldn't miss your wedding! So it's going to be in Japan?"

"Yes. Really, just his immediate family and mine. I'd love for you to come here so we could go dress shopping, but Hai's family is Shinto, so I think I'm going to wear a *shiro-muko.* So it's probably better if Hai's mom helps me pick it out."

"All right," Diana said, thought she wasn't quite sure what that was. Truthfully, she'd never pictured Bea in a white gown. She'd long since known that giving Bea advice was futile—the free-spirited girl did whatever she liked. And as long as Bea was happy, Diana didn't care. Clearly, from Bea's chipper tone of voice, she was still ecstatic from the engagement ring she'd gotten, a few days before. "Sounds lovely. Let me know if I can help with anything."

"Okay, Mommy. Have fun at *Musikhoffen,* or whatever you said."

"*Musikverein.*"

"Right! That, too. Love you."

"Love you, too."

She hung up and realized she had another text from Lily: *Mick's having a fit. I was in such a rush to pack that I think I left the earrings he gave me for our anniversary in the bathroom of the AirBNB we rented in Verona. Do you know the number of them, so I can call?*

Diana sighed and typed in: *I'm so sorry. But I don't have that info. Your father rented the place, remember? Ask him.*

A moment later: *Oh, right! Thanks! I'll check with him.*

She shook her head. Lily had always been the book-smart one, but she lacked common sense, sometimes. Thus, believing in ax murderers, and often losing and forgetting things when she went on trips. And messaging her mother, who was in another country, instead of her father, who was clearly better equipped to help her with this situation. Not that Evan had ever been very good at helping the kids with their "situations." Diana had always been the fix-it parent.

But it had always been that way, with everything. Her daughters had always been closer to her than they'd been to Evan.

But they can do without me for one night.

She flipped the phone to Do-Not-Disturb and checked the time. Fifteen minutes until her reservation, and then, at eight, she'd be in the hall that had witnessed some of the greatest music ever played. She couldn't wait. She grabbed her purse and headed out the door.

Don't worry, Diana. It's good to be alone. No one to bother you. You can really concentrate on your food. On the music. You'll have tears in your eyes before long!

Two hours and counting. Soon, the magic would begin. She wondered if she would even be able to enjoy the meal prior, with the excitement swirling in her stomach.

CHAPTER FIVE

When Diana's cab pulled up at the restaurant, she looked across the street at *Musikverein* and a chill passed through her. There it was: the hallowed hall of the greatest musicians known to man. She stared up at it, reading the words, *Gesellschaft der Musikfreunde,* wondering what that meant. A lot of German was similar to English. Friends of music? Well, that was definitely her.

Similar to the café, the Restaurant Ludwig on Dumbastraße/Bösendorferstraße, though conjuring up images of instruments and sheet music and everything Beethoven, had no décor whatsoever to show that it was connected with the famous music hall across the street. As Diana walked into the modern restaurant with geometrical patterns on the wall and tables with stark white cloths, she decided that the gimmick of adding memorabilia to the walls of a restaurant to convey a cutesy theme was perhaps more of an American thing. As the waiter led her to her table, a booth in the corner, and she shuffled around the long, curved bench seating, she realized she'd have very little of interest to look at while she dined.

Not to mention, the booth felt rather cavernous for her, alone. She had plenty of room at her elbows. It almost felt as though it was swallowing her up.

"Enjoy your meal," the host said as he placed a menu in front of her.

She took a sip of the water in front of her as she studied the offerings on the menu. As she did, a woman across the way giggled. Diana looked up to see a buxom, scantily-dressed blonde woman with an older man who seemed completely entranced by her. She couldn't help but think of Evan and his fiancé, Tilda, who was Bea's age. Evan and Tilda looked ridiculous together, more like father and daughter, probably to everyone but themselves.

But as she scanned the restaurant, she realized there were quite a few gray-haired or bald men with their attractive, younger significant others.

The point was, at least they were *together*. And they all seemed to be having a lovely time.

Leaving Diana, and all the other women who'd reached their fifties, to sit alone in restaurant corners, drowning their sorrows in wiener schnitzel and beer and watching them having the time of their lives.

She may have been over men, but sometimes, only sometimes . . . she had to admit, they had their charm.

The waiter came and said, "All alone, are we?"

"Yes," she stated, a little flatly, though just minutes ago, she'd resolved not to let it bother her. *Thanks for pointing that out.*

"That's all right," he said, as if there was something intrinsically wrong with it, but he needed to be polite. "Would you like to hear our specials?"

"No, thanks," she said, now wanting to finish up and leave as quickly as possible. She scanned the menu and chose the first thing that caught her eye. "I'll have the wiener schnitzel. And a glass of your house white. Thanks."

He nodded, took the menu from her, and left.

She sighed, still watching Blondie and her older companion, heads tilted toward one another, whispering sweet nothings in each other's ear. She took a forkful of something and fed it to him, giggling when he tasted it. They were so involved in one another; Diana didn't have to worry about openly gawking—they wouldn't have noticed her if her hair caught fire. She flashed back to the times when Evan had taken her out to fancy dinners in New York, and they'd looked that way, so completely oblivious to everything and everyone around them.

It had been a long, *long* time. She could barely remember it. It felt like another lifetime.

But it was okay. She done all that before. She'd fallen in love, and two lovely children had come out of it. Her marriage had been good, but it wasn't without its troubles. There was something to be said about being alone, having no one to answer to but yourself. *Had I been here with a man, I might not have had the nerve to order something as fattening as the wiener schnitzel—I might have forced myself to go with JUST a salad. And what fun would that be?*

The waiter came by with her first course, and she laid the napkin on her lap and dug in. *Salad's not bad when you have more coming. I don't even have to worry about getting salad dressing on my chin! This is freeing!* She thought to herself.

Then Blondie giggled loudly. She looked over to see them, glasses raised, toasting each other.

Diana stared at her as the older man lifted her hand and lovingly kissed her knuckles.

She sighed and took a large mouthful of her salad. *I need to get out of here before I get sick. Quickly.*

As she was sucking a piece of radicchio into her mouth, coated with vinaigrette, someone came and stood in front of her. "Fancy meeting you here."

Vinaigrette splashed on her face. She looked up to see the large, round form of the man she'd seen earlier, in the park. The one with the pants that went up to his breastbone. Now, he was wearing a dinner jacket that hid that particular wardrobe calamity, but he was still wearing his jaunty Tyrolean hat. He took it off and bowed to her, as low as he could go for his substantial weight, which was only a few inches at most.

"Oh. Uh . . . hi . . . "

"Hans."

"Right. How are you?"

"Very good, thanks. And you are?"

She looked around. "Fine. I'm Diana."

He grasped her hand, bowing again and pressing a wet kiss to her knuckles before she could think to pull it away. When she did, she saw slobber, in the shape of his mouth, there. She wiped it on her napkin, finding a bit of brown vinaigrette there, too.

"I see you are dining alone. I am dining alone, too. Perhaps we dine together?"

"Well, I—"

He slid in so that, in order to get away from his massive form, she had no choice but to shuffle over to the other edge of the bench. As he set his big form down, the bench groaned in protest and her cushion inflated underneath her, see-sawing her up a little bit. The crystal and silverware bounced on the table, and she had to grab her wine to stop it from sloshing over the side of the glass.

Suddenly, the once-cavernous booth felt very cramped, indeed. His large belly strained against the table, looking like a balloon that was on the verge of popping. "The goulash here is particularly *wunderbar*, might I recommend."

She frowned and pointed to her salad. "I've already ordered."

"Ah! So you did!" He grinned and patted his hefty stomach. "I can't eat the salad. It doesn't agree with me."

She nodded. "Yes. I understand," she said, even though she didn't. She scanned the tables in front of her, and all the people, making pleasant conversation. Maybe that was all she needed to do. Converse pleasantly with him. It didn't have to be romantic. In fact, romance was the last thing she wanted. "So, are you from Vienna?"

He shook his head. "From Innsbruck. So you are American? I have been there once. I like your Longhorn Steak House."

"Right. What part did you visit?"

"Oh, I was just there for business. They had a great buffet breakfast. At the Waffle House?"

"Yes. Right. What kind of business are you in?"

"I finance things. We all had dinner at the. . . . the Shoney's? Yes? That is good food, right there."

Yes, America is known for its "fine" dining, for sure. She sighed and looked around. Why did it seem like forever since the waiter had taken her order? "I'm sorry, Hans. But you know, you might want to eat elsewhere. Remember that performance I was trying to get a ticket to? I was able to snag one."

"At *Musikverein*? That's a feat. Good for you!" His eyes narrowed. "Not from one of those thieves, I hope?"

"Oh no. I should thank you, because you were right. The scalper's prices were outrageous. I was able to get the ticket from a woman who was unable to attend. So it all worked out."

She pushed her salad away, no longer hungry, as he said, "And what is on the program for tonight?"

"Oh . . . it's Lukas Huber."

"Ah." He frowned, opened his mouth to speak, but seemed to think better of it, because his fleshy jaw snapped shut. Was it possible she'd finally found the one Austrian who wasn't in love with the pianist? Or maybe he just wasn't interested in classical. "And what will the philharmonic be performing tonight?"

"I believe, from what I read, it's Schubert's Unfinished, Beethoven's 4th Piano Concerto, and an original composition from Huber himself that has never before been performed. The Jupiter Symphony."

He grunted. "Ah, the two friends! Never can go wrong with Schubert's 8th. And Beethoven's 4th is a good one. You know that both were performed for the first time in Vienna?"

She nodded. Well, she knew half of that.

"And you can visit their graves at *Zentralfriedhof,* here? Schubert, Beethoven, the Strausses, Brahms . . . they are all buried here in the city."

She nodded, unsure. She might have considered it, but she'd done something similar in Paris and wasn't sure she wanted to make her year in Europe a grave-finding trip. It sounded too morbid.

"But Huber . . . I find him a bit too heavy-handed for my liking." He stroked his double chin. "You know, a musician's demeanor is as original as a fingerprint. The untrained ear may hear a piece of music and say, well, it is Brahms. Or it is Beethoven. And Beethoven is Beethoven. But musician interpretation is everything. And a matter of opinion. Huber is popular, just not my cup of tea. He seems to—how shall I say? Dally. I don't see that he has a particular style. Some say Liszt, but I think that's just his demeanor. He's popular with the ladies."

That wasn't the first time she'd heard that. "Maybe you can answer a question I was wondering about. What do the words on front of the *Musikverein* mean?"

"Gesellschaft der Musikfreunde? It translates roughly to 'Society for the Friends of Music.'"

"Oh, interesting." She scrabbled for her phone. "Anyway, I'm in a bit of a rush because I should be getting to the music hall in a bit. I don't want to be late for the performance."

"That's all right. You can leave at any time," he said, unconcerned, as the waiter came by with a place setting for him. He unfolded the napkin and stuck one corner into the collar of his shirt, like a bib. Then he said to the waiter, *"Wiener schnitzel. Und Kalbsrahmbeuschel."*

Diana didn't even want to know what that was. At that moment, her wiener schnitzel came, golden fried, with a heaping helping of fries. It smelled heavenly, which was good, because Hans brought with him the stench of stale beer and something sour.

"Really, though," she said, wondering if she could lie, make up a husband that had "left to use the restroom?" Excuse *herself* to use the restroom, then climb out a window? Pretend to choke on a fry and get carted off to the hospital? None of her ideas seemed feasible. "It's quite crowded here. Don't you think you might be more comfortable somewhere else?"

He chuckled. "How could I be? Here, I am in the company of the most beautiful woman in the place."

Then he put his hand, meaty and sweaty, on hers.

Horrified, she snatched it away. He clearly wasn't getting the picture. He reached over, and without asking, grabbed a fry from her plate and tossed it in his mouth. Maybe he'd paid her the compliment, just so she'd let him have one. She took a fry and bit into it, then checked her phone again.

"Oh. Wow. It is getting late!" It wasn't, really, but even if she got there early, she was sure she'd find a lot to explore at *Musikverein*. She motioned to the waiter. "Check, please."

She noticed that he made no offer to pay for her. Not that she wanted him to. In fact, she would've been fine if she never saw him again, the rest of her time in Austria. She quickly handed her credit card over to the waiter, counting the moments until he returned, as Hans told her some story about the first *Kalbsrahmbeuschel* he'd ever had, made by his grandmother in Bischofshofen when he was only a lad. Apparently, it was some kind of food, and apparently, it had been love at first taste.

She quickly signed the check and pocketed her card, then sprang up. Hans struggled to, too, which was actually gentlemanly of him, but then he gave up the fight and settled back down. He picked up one of her fries. "You're not eating this?"

She shook her head. "No. Sorry. I've got to go."

"Mind if I . . ." He was already picking up a fork and licking his lips as he gazed at it.

"No. Knock yourself out. It was nice talking to you," she said. "Maybe I will see you around somewhere."

He said something that might have been *Enjoy the concert,* but his mouth was already full of food.

When she got outside, she gulped the fresh air and sighed. Funny; just when she'd been lamenting dining alone, the universe happened to drop Hans on her. *Well played, universe.* If that wasn't a reminder to just be happy with her own company, she didn't know what was.

As she prepared to cross the street, she looked back at the restaurant. In another life, not long ago, she'd been a Marketing Director at one of the biggest cosmetics companies in New York, unafraid of being a lioness, often telling people what to do and ruffling feathers for the good of the company. But when it came to telling people what to do *for her own good,* she was more like a mouse. She'd spent nearly half an hour in that man's company, completely miserable, when she should've just told him that she wasn't interested.

"I need to get some more backbone," she murmured aloud, turning to stare at her reflection in the glass window of the restaurant. She looked utterly flustered. "You're a grown woman. Learn to stand up for yourself, Dear."

As she was staring at her reflection, she happened to look past it and see Hans, mouth full, cheeks on the verge of popping, waving excitedly at her. The table in front of him was full of plates of food. Had he ordered one of everything after she left?

Standing under the overhang, she noticed it'd begun to drizzle. She reached for the umbrella she kept in her bag, but after a moment's thought, pulled out her itinerary. Grabbing her pen, underneath *Be moved to tears by beautiful music,* she wrote, *Stand up for yourself!*

She underlined it a few times, then pocketed it before opening her umbrella. People were beginning to crowd toward the music hall, stepping through scattered puddles and dodging raindrops as they went. Diana followed them, promising herself that the next time she was in an uncomfortable situation, she'd speak her mind.

But right now, it was time to let the music move her.

CHAPTER SIX

Diana spun around inside the Golden Hall of *Musikverein,* hardly able to believe she was there.

She'd seen the gilded, ornate walls of the theater every year, while watching the New Year's Concert on PBS. The long, glimmering, shoebox-shaped hall was so opulent and cheerful, bordered on each side by high balconies. Every surface was an explosion of scrollwork and color, and fresh flowers burst from vases everywhere. Above, ten great, glittering chandeliers filled the room with abundant light. The seats on the floor, though, were the best ones. So she was shocked when the usher led her to a seat in the center aisle, only a few rows from the stage. She scanned the stage, her eyes going all the way up the wall beyond it, to the massive pipes of an organ. Above her, frescos of angels were painted on the ceiling, a detail she hadn't noticed while watching this on television.

"Enjoy," the young usher said as he pointed her toward her seat.

She practically skipped over to the row and stood there, checking her distance from the seat to the stage. It was so close; she could almost reach out and touch the grand piano in the center of it. "I'm sure I will!"

He grinned at her, clearly amused by her obvious excitement. He was probably not much older than eighteen, his face still dotted with acne, tall, but skeletal and lanky. The usher's dapper three-piece tux didn't do much to age him. "It's quite a place, eh?" he said, and even his voice had a bit of a prepubescent squeak to it.

She nodded.

"And the acoustics are even better. Just you wait. I know. I dreamed of working here when I was a kid, just like Brahms had. Now, I finally do. Started here when I was sixteen, but I still come to work excited, every day. I love it here." He looked around, pride shining in his eyes, like a child showing off his bedroom trophy collection. "And you have one of the best seats in the house!"

"You think?"

"Sure. If you're too close, you can't see the whole orchestra. Too far away, and you wouldn't be able to see the magic the pianist does with his fingers. From that seat, you can see it all! In fact, if I had to pick any seat in the place, it would be that one there."

"Oh, thank you!" She clapped her hands together in excitement.

I can't believe I'm finally here! How many other things have I not noticed while watching on my television set? This place is bigger than I thought. The seats are smaller. And I bet the music will sound a million times better in person!

Her seat was three in, in row four. As she squeezed around a man and woman, saying "Excuse me," she gazed at the stage. It was so close, she could almost reach out and touch the performers. She settled into her seat, then opened the program and read a little about all of the performers and the Vienna Philharmonic. The conductor was new to the Philharmonic, though he had an impressive list of credentials, but the person she zeroed in on was Lukas Huber himself.

The photograph of him was stunning—he was older than she'd expected, maybe in his early forties. He had long dark hair that fell upon his shoulders, a pronounced, strong jaw coated in stubble, and though his eyes were as dark as coal, he gazed at the camera in a way that smoldered. She'd heard of his talent, but she hadn't expected him to be so, well, attractive.

She read his bio:

Lukas Huber is a composer and pianist virtuoso from Vienna, Austria. He was born in Innsbruck, and began studying the piano when he was only five years old. He studied music in Salzburg and in Montreal.

His career took a major leap when he won the 2005 international competition in Carnegie Hall. Ever since then, he has been recording and performing around the world. Apart from his work as a first-rate pianist, Huber is renowned for his admirable composing skills. His compositions include a set of many symphonies and piano etudes, which have been performed all over the world. Tonight, he is excited to bring to you his most ambitious work yet, the grand Jupiter Symphony. Jupiter, God of Thunder and Sky, is King of Gods, and according to Huber himself, "This symphony suggests pure power on a massive scale, harnessed, in musical form."

His work is notably comparable to the great Franz Liszt, according to many critics, but hints of Beethoven, Bach, and Mozart can also be found in his unique and inspired compositions.

She looked up, even more excited, at the gorgeous Bösendorfer Grand piano that was only a few yards away from her. In just a few minutes, he'd be *right there.* Almost close enough to touch!

The hall continued to fill up, everyone dressed to the nines, in a way that made Diana feel underdressed, even in the fanciest dress in her suitcase. They all looked as if they were about to attend a Long Island wedding—the men in suits, the women in gowns or tea-length dresses.

Diana moved her legs aside to let another couple sit to her right.

"*Entschuldigung*!" the woman said as she stepped on Diana's toe.

Diana winced and looked up, and realized that it was Blondie, from the restaurant. *Of course it is. With my luck, they'll start making out during the performance.*

She flounced down next to Diana, smelling so strongly of some perfume that it made Diana's eyes water. From here, even though she didn't want to, Diana could see right into the cleavage of her tight-fitting spaghetti-strap gown. She tossed her blonde mane playfully, slapping Diana in the face with her curls, and said, "Oooh, Gunther. What songs are they going to play?"

Diana fought the urge to roll her eyes. The young woman reminded her so much of Evan's fiancé, Tilda, better known as Vidal, since she was all about her hair. But in Verona, she and Tilda had come to an understanding, and in the end, Diana had given Tilda and Evan her blessing and wished them well. Sometimes that was the best thing to do—just let go.

So when the woman hogged her armrest, Diana closed her eyes and tried to channel that feeling.

Forgive. Feel the calmness and clarity of letting go.

She reached into her bag, pulled out her itinerary, and wrote that down underneath *Stand up for yourself!*

Of course, the two things had to war with one another. Part of her wanted to forgive Vidal Part Two for stepping on her toe and constantly slapping her with her sweet-smelling locks. And part of her wanted to scream, *Do you mind?*

But she didn't have time to do either. A moment later, the lights dimmed, signaling the show was about to begin. The chatter died to an absolute silence. When the lights came back on again, the musicians began to file into the rows on the stage and pick up their instruments. Some of them tuned them, others looked at their music.

Diana held her breath as a tall man in a tuxedo and tails walked out—the concertmaster. He watched and listened as the other members of the orchestra tuned their instruments. Diana watched closely. *This is another thing they never show you on PBS!*

When he finished with the other members of the orchestra, he picked up his own violin, and the violinists followed suit, tuning their instruments. When complete, the notes died down.

Then, the conductor walked out, to loud applause.

He bowed, stood at his podium besides the piano, tapped his wand, and the orchestra began to play.

The music filled the hall, easily proving why this hall was renowned above all others. Despite the quiet start, the acoustics were lovely. It was another one of her favorite pieces, Schubert's Symphony No. 8, the Unfinished Symphony. Only two movements long, it was unforgettable; it had always stuck with her. At times, when listening to this music with her grandmother, she'd felt very moved by the beauty of it. It started simply, with the cellos in the background providing a nervous shimmer, before the oboe and clarinet came in, playing a lilting, haunting melody over the murmuring strings.

Diana felt goosebumps popping up, all over her bare arms. Beautiful, but not quite enough to move her to tears. She often felt close to crying, even watching the orchestra on television, as the violinists swayed to the melodies, bows moving in unison, getting lost in their music. Now, she felt closer, but not quite there. Not enough to be able to cross the item off her bucket list. *Maybe I want it too much.*

The first movement came to an end. The music hall fell into absolute silence. No one even coughed or moved. It was always hard, during those between-movement times, after hearing something so beautiful, to fight the urge to applaud wildly. She moved to the edge of her seat, waiting for the next and final movement to begin.

As she did, there came a loud, instantly recognizable tinkling sound, from somewhere off stage. Diana shook her head as the tune went on.

Oh, for goodness sake! Some idiot forgot to silence their phone.

People looked around, trying to figure out where the sound was coming from. Even the conductor dropped his raised hands and looked over his shoulder.

It was *The Entertainer*, coming from somewhere very nearby. Diana stiffened. *I've heard that before.*

The thought hit her an instant later: *Of course you have, dummy. That idiot is you! It's YOUR phone!*

Diana jumped to action, grabbing her phone from her purse and switching it to silent. Hadn't she done that before? She was sure she had, but she must've pushed the wrong button.

Next to her, the blonde woman glared and let out a groan of disgust. "Do you mind?" she said, her voice dripping with irritation. She leaned in to whisper something to her beau, that sounded like, *Some people have no class.*

Forgive. Feel the calmness and clarity of letting go, she thought, gritting her teeth and warding off the desire to elbow the woman in the boobs.

When she finally silenced the phone, heat growing in her cheeks, she looked around at her companions, who were all staring at her with indignation, and mouthed, *I'm sorry.*

The music went on. By then, Diana was too embarrassed to get into the music. Eventually, though, the chagrin faded, and she was able to close her eyes and let the melody carry her away. She felt it lift her troubles from her shoulders and relax her, as it always had when she'd curled up on the rug of her grandmother's living room. Here she was, in the greatest music hall on Earth, listening to the greatest orchestra on Earth. Could there be anything better?

But no tears.

Not a single one.

When the symphony ended, Diana applauded loudly, along with everyone else. The conductor nodded to the audience, then presented the orchestra, then nodded again. When the applause died down, he left the stage.

The next time the conductor walked out, he was not alone. With him was the startlingly handsome man Diana recognized from his photograph in the program.

Lukas Huber.

He's here! Diana thought. *The next Beethoven! Here it comes. Now I am definitely going to hear music that will move me to tears!*

CHAPTER SEVEN

Dressed in a tux with gray cravat, Lukas Huber smiled self-assuredly, a bit of a swagger in his walk. He didn't appear the least bit nervous or even concentrated on his work, as many virtuosos often did prior to a performance. In fact, whereas most performers wanted to get the show on the road, Lukas Huber seemed to delight in the applause, as if he would've been fine with it continuing and delaying his performance indefinitely. He even waved. The applause continued on, until Diana wondered if the performance would ever begin.

Then he lifted his tails and sat at the Bösendorfer Grand piano. Diana shifted in her seat to get a good look at him around the heads of the other people in front of her in the audience. He nodded to the conductor, placed his hands on the keys, bent low to the piano, and began to play, quietly at first.

The conductor lifted his hands, and the violins joined in, answering the piano's melody. It was a balanced dialogue between the instrument and the rest of the orchestra, sometimes lively, sometimes mournful.

Diana listened, hardly able to breathe, thinking of the way her grandparents used to love this concerto. And this rendition was by far the best one she'd ever heard. Watching Huber there, live, right in front of her, as his hands masterfully caressed the keys, was astounding. She always wondered how pianists could play such long pieces without the music in front of them, but it was a testament to how well-rehearsed and talented they were. He went on, eyes closed, swaying to the music, his fingers working a frenzy on the keys, sometimes moving so fast that it was impossible to see them. It was awe-inspiring, certainly.

And yet still . . . no tears.

This is amazing. Why am I not crying? Is something wrong with me?

She listened through the remaining movements, and applauded with everyone else at the end. By the time it was over, it seemed impossible to think that Huber would be able to play his own arrangement. But after a short pause to bow and smile and wave for the crowd, he sat back down and began to play. This was it. The debut of his Jupiter

Symphony, the piece of music that will light the classical music world on fire.

It's history being made. Of course, this will make me cry. I'm sure of it.

And again, it was lovely. Very moving. He seemed to care greatly for the work, and the melody was haunting, combining with that of the oboe, to create a truly mournful sound that pulled at Diana's heartstrings. She listened intently, not wanting to look away, not even wanting to breathe, for fear of missing something.

Still, no tears.

But he's wonderful. Amazing. I'd love to have his autograph, because he's probably the best in the world. And yet . . . why did I not cry?

As the last note lingered in the hall, Diana realized that it was over. Over, and her eyes had stayed completely dry. People jumped to their feet in a standing ovation. Diana followed them, applauding until her hands hurt. Huber stood up and swaggered to the edge of the stage, where he again smiled broadly and bowed for the audience. Waved some more, and even winked at a few people. Then he strutted off the stage as the applause continued.

Diana watched him go as the rest of the orchestra began to leave. When she looked up at the stage, she realized with a sinking feeling that that was it.

She lingered there, not wanting to let it go. Her last, best chance.

Here she was, in the greatest hall on Earth, with the greatest performer on Earth, and she'd missed her chance. She cursed herself for letting her phone go off. She cursed herself for being too nervous to fully get into the music and let it take her away. It wasn't the venue, or the performers. They were clearly celebrated and deserved to be so. No, this was something else. Whatever happened, she felt like it was her fault.

Maybe it was because I was here all alone. I couldn't let myself relax enough to just enjoy it.

She gathered her things as the theater patrons began to leave. As she was walking up the aisles toward the back of the hall, she noticed a couple of women, slipping behind some curtains that seemed to lead toward some back room. *I wonder if I could go in there and actually meet him?*

She glanced around. Most people seemed intent on the exit doors. No one appeared to be lingering. No one would notice her if she just slipped off, to the side, would they?

You only live once. And you're only at Musikverein once in a blue moon, she said, side-stepping over to the curtains. Once she got close enough, she scurried to it, ripped the curtain back, and slipped inside, finding herself in a long hallway.

The second she got there, she had a strange sense of déjà vu. It was only a week ago that she'd gone to visit a handsome actor backstage in Verona, only to witness his poisoning. That had been the start of a crazy few days of trying to prove her innocence while finding out who the real killer was. But this time, she wasn't interested in love. All she wanted was to meet the "Next Beethoven," tell him how wonderful he was, and get his autograph on her program. Simple.

She followed the women down the narrow hallway, toward the back of the stage. When she turned a corner, the hallway opened up to a larger hallway, which was choked with people, mostly women. They were all murmuring and chanting, "Lukas!" Someone let out a squeal of, "I love you, Lukas!"

Apparently, Diana wasn't the only one with the idea of meeting him after the show. It was just as Leonie Winkler had said—people were lined up to meet him, waving their hands frantically in effort to get his attention. They all seemed to be zeroed in on him, but Diana couldn't see. Diana tried to stand on her tip-toes, but all of the women were also on their toes, trying to get a better look. Some of them had their arms raised, and were waving their programs. Others had rolled posters and . . . wait, was that woman holding her lace underwear?

One woman shouted, *"Ich liebe dich, Lukas!"* Another followed. Diana assumed that was some version of, *I love you, Lukas!*

An older woman next to Diana fanned her ruddy face. "I can't believe it. I can't believe I am so close to him. He's so beautiful, like some kind of Greek god."

Diana looked at her. "Does he get this kind of reaction all the time?"

She nodded. "Oh, yes. And it's only growing! Oh, he's so sexy."

A younger woman jumped and whistled, then screamed, "I will have your children, Lukas Huber! Call me!" just as the ruddy-faced woman let out a gasp of air.

Diana turned to her in horror as she slowly slipped to her knees, then slumped face first on the ground, right at Diana's feet.

CHAPTER EIGHT

Diana blinked. *Seriously. People do have a way of falling at your feet, don't they, Diana?*

Meanwhile, nobody else seemed to notice this poor woman had sprawled onto the marble floor, out cold, her dress up around her thighs to reveal part of a lace slip. They were too busy jumping up and down, trying to meet their idol. Was this a classical music performance or a Beatles concert?

She knelt down to check on the woman, whose eyelids fluttered. She murmured, "Lukas, Lukas, Lukas . . . are you there, my love?" in her delirium.

Diana put a hand on her ruddy cheek and turned her face upward, trying to get her to focus. "Hello? Are you okay?"

The woman continued to murmur. The crowd, oblivious to them, swelled larger, until it started to swallow them up. She pulled the woman onto her lap as someone's massive purse knocked against the back of Diana's head. "Hello?" She patted her cheeks a little more forcefully.

The woman's eyes fluttered open and she stared at Diana. "Who are you? Where am I? Where's Lukas?"

"I—" Someone stepped on Diana's heel and didn't bother to say "Excuse me;" in fact, it seemed like the crowd was so obsessed with Lukas Huber that none would've noticed if a nuclear bomb went off in the building next to them.

We're about to get trampled, Diana thought with worry as she held the woman's unnaturally cold and clammy hand. *I've got to get her out of here.*

"Uh . . . ambulance?" she called, standing up, reaching for the phone in her purse. "Can I get an ambulance, here?"

Just then, two security guards in gray uniforms, one male, one female, arrived. The woman was clearly upset. "What . . . wasn't anyone watching the doors? Where did all these people come from?"

"You know Huber. He insists on us letting them back here," the male guard said, and spoke into a radio. "We need more help back here," he said, and attempted to corral the growing crowd.

Diana waved to him. "Help, please help. This woman fainted."

The female guard rolled her eyes. "Of course she did. Happens all the time. George! We've got another fainter!"

Together, the three of them were able to lift the woman up and get her to a bench at the side of the hallway. By then, she was awake and alert, yet no less starstruck. She clutched her program in a sweaty death-grip. "I have to get my program signed by Lukas. It is a dream for me! I came here all the way from *Schruns!*"

Diana had no idea where that was, but she felt sorry for the poor woman. More guards had arrived, and were beginning to get the crowd under control. Some people were leaving of their own free will, but a few were lingering, still trying to see the great pianist. As the commotion died down, Diana could hear the man speaking, loudly and confidently, though she couldn't make out his words. The women in his circle, though, now a comfortable grouping of fifteen to twenty, were all listening, rapt. She moved closer.

"He's so *wunderbar*," a woman gushed dreamily.

Diana watched their faces. They couldn't have been more captivated had Lukas Huber hypnotized them. In fact, he *had* hypnotized them. Diana watched for a few moments, and never saw one of them blink.

Suddenly, a couple of women broke through the group, giggling. "I got his signature! Right here!" She pointed out the scrawl on the front of her program.

The other woman dipped her blouse to show a scrawl over her cleavage. "I got one, here." She patted her heart, swooning. "Oh, my goodness. I am never going to wash again! He's so sexy!"

The two women skipped off like schoolgirls after talking to their first crush. Now, it was much more orderly, with the guards guiding people toward the exit once they finished speaking with Huber. A few other people peeled away from the group, heading off with their own signatures. Diana watched them, summoning her courage. *Well, why not?*

She went back to the fainting woman and took her program. "Stay here. I'll get our programs signed. Okay?"

"You will?" The woman's eyes filled with excitement. "Oh, thank you."

Diana moved into the crowd, behind a woman with her young son. She maneuvered so she could see the man of the hour better. Huber was even more good-looking in person; he was actually quite slim and small in stature, but with his long dark hair, a bit windswept like Beethoven's, and dark stubble framing a sparkling white smile, he had a certain charm about him. As Diana swayed this way and that, trying to get a better look, he held a program and signed it, meanwhile, talking in a voice that leaked confidence, bordering on arrogance. Something about it triggered another bout of déjà vu. The way he spoke, he reminded her of someone . . .

It was only when she'd gotten close enough to get a perfect view of him that she actually listened to his words. He was speaking to a woman with a lot of dark hair and too much make-up. She was one of those types who would've been beautiful without make-up, tall and dark-skinned and high-cheekboned. Diana was sure she'd seen her, sitting a couple rows in front of her. The thick mane of ebony curls gave her away.

"Well, evidently, *liebchen.* But while I have taken a bit of inspiration from Beethoven, the truth is that he wasn't the most gifted musician. He lacked style. I've taken something from the greats, here and there, but you can't deny that I've improved upon it. As you could tell by my Jupiter Symphony. It was stunning, yes?"

Diana just stared at him. Had he just said what she thought he said? That he was a better musician than Beethoven? Right.

She nearly laughed at the absurdity. He must've just misspoken. He couldn't have meant that. And The Jupiter Symphony had sounded nice, but . . .

"Why did you choose to call it that?"

He chuckled. "Because Jupiter is the best, of course."

The beautiful woman at his elbow leaned into him and whispered something in his ear. He smiled with delight and murmured something back to her. There was some familiarity there. She had to wonder if they'd been acquainted before.

The young woman with the child was now next to Diana. She leaned in to Diana and whispered, "This is the greatest day of my son, Franz's life. He is a big fan. We've come here from Innsbruck to meet him. I saved up all year so I could purchase these tickets for his birthday. He has wanted to meet him, his whole life!"

"Oh, how wonderful," Diana said back to her, excited to see the boy's dream come true.

Huber signed another program for someone and said, "Yes, well. I know, some journalist somewhere compared me to Liszt, and another called me the Next Beethoven, but they're philistines, really. The two composers are clearly different as night and day, and have their own thumbprint, as I have mine. How can you put me in a place between the two? Let the reporters write their banal puff pieces for the masses, as long as it sells papers. I'd like to think of my work as in a class of its own."

"Well, what piece of classical music is your favorite?" someone from the crowd asked.

"Honestly?" He grinned and shrugged humbly. "Mine! I'm partial to my Jupiter. It was wonderful, was it not?"

Everyone broke out in laughter, clearly agreeing with him.

"But truly, they're like my children. I can't possibly choose from among them. Really. The traditional composers clearly had a lot of talent. But their efforts are rudimentary. I added new layers, new depth that's never been seen before. In fact, Riccardo Muti, the great conductor, just told me that of all the works he's ever had the privilege of conducting, mine are the most challenging, just because of their intensity. And I have to agree. I challenge my orchestra. As it should be."

The woman in front of Diana nudged her son forward and said, meekly, "Mr. Huber. My son, Franz, has been playing piano since he was three. You are one of his idols, and—"

"Yes, yes," he muttered, winking at a blonde in the crowd. "Don't just stand there skulking behind your mommy's legs, boy. Give me your damn program and let me sign it."

With shaking fingers, the child, who couldn't have been more than ten, held the program out. Huber grabbed it, scribbled something, and tossed it back to the boy.

"Now go home. It's after your bedtime. Time for the adults to play." He gave the women in the audience a mischievous glance.

The poor kid, head down, retreated, without so much as another word. Diana looked after him, feeling sorry for him, as he let out a big sob, broke through the crowd, and rushed off.

His mother ran after him. He'd learned a big lesson. *Never meet your heroes. They're sure to disappoint you.*

Meanwhile, the blowhard Huber continued, unaffected by the child's clear disappointment. Had he even noticed, or had his big ego been blocking the way? "Schubert's fine, and everything. But he really was just a mole, sitting in Beethoven's shadow all his life. He really had to work hard to achieve anything with his stilted tunes . . . I still say that's why his eighth symphony went unfinished . . ."

Now he was saying he was superior to Schubert? Was there anyone in this world he was inferior to? Diana couldn't help it. Though she meant to cover her mouth, she wound up letting out a laugh.

Of course, at that moment, Huber decided to come up for air from his long-winded speech, so there was relative silence for her laugh. Everyone turned toward her. Huber snapped his eyes to her. "What? What do you know about great music, woman?"

"Well, yours was good, but—"

"Of course it was! Mine was incomparable," he said smugly. "Wait . . . I know you. You're the woman in the audience whose phone went off during the performance. *The Entertainer*, hmm?"

A general gasp rose up from the crowd. People looked at her with disgust.

"And you want to critique my musical genius? You have some nerve!" He said, looking around and smiling at his admirers.

Her cheeks burned with indignation. Fighting the urge to run off, she blurted, "It's not a critique. More of an observation. You mentioned that your work challenges the orchestra. But is that really the aim of musical composition?"

He frowned. "What are you saying?"

Now, the crowd had gone silent. Everyone was looking at her. Her cheeks flamed more, the heat travelling down the back of her neck. "I'm just saying that good music doesn't have to be complicated. It's more than that. So much more. It should transport. Transform." *Move someone to tears.*

He scoffed. "Mine does that."

Suddenly, it occurred to her just why her sense of déjà vu seemed to be growing, the more she spoke with this man. She'd had an awful blowhard of a professor at college in New York, in one of her history classes. Professor Marsden. He was a total jerk, who loved the sound of his own voice. He'd get up to the podium and pontificate for the entire class, never bother to answer questions, and if anyone wanted to debate him on any point, he'd shut them down. When someone didn't know an answer, he'd make fun of them. Unless, of course, it was a pretty girl. Professor Marsden always had an eye for the pretty girls, and would often ask them to stay after, using his influence and stature in the college to prey on them.

The thought made her stomach turn. She said, not really sure what she was getting at, "Maybe it does. But you can't say that the others were inferior just because they were less complicated. A whole bunch of notes can be just that—a whole bunch of notes. And yet a single note, played in just the right way, can be all you need." She thought about what her grandmother used to say, about some of her favorite pieces. "Sometimes, simplicity is better."

He snorted, as if the notion was ridiculous.

It probably was. Why was she even talking to him about this? She knew nothing about music. She was a casual listener, which was far from a serious performer. But somehow, her wayward mouth betrayed her. "It's true."

He stared at her, his face twisting with rage. "What's your name?"

Oh no. Now you're in for it. This is where Professor Marsden would embarrass you out of the room. "Diana. Diana St. James."

To her surprise, a smile appeared on his face. He motioned her forward. "Come. Come here. Let her through."

The people on either side of her parted, allowing her an easy path to him. She squeezed through, trying to keep her breathing even.

"American?"

She nodded.

Then he pointed to the programs in her hand. "You want those signed?"

She nodded and handed them to him. But he just stared at them, then motioned her closer.

Diana moved closer. He motioned her even closer, so close that she was almost touching him, as if he wanted to tell her a secret.

He leaned in, his breath hot on her ear as he cupped a hand around his mouth and held it to her. "I'll sign those programs for you if you agree to meet me in the alley out back for a little fun. Shall we say, ten o'clock?"

Her jaw dropped. She pulled away from him in revulsion.

He smiled and looked her up and down. “You’re older than I’m used to, but you’re still a looker. Plus, I like the old ones. They know what they want. What do you say, woman?”

She stared, speechless for a while, her face growing redder and redder. She turned, meaning to stomp away, but she knew she wouldn’t feel fulfilled if she left, now. She was just too angry. Besides, how many times had she’d wished she could be in Professor Marsden’s presence now, to give him a piece of her mind without having to worry about him giving her an F because of it?

Men like that *needed* to be put in their place.

And right then, Diana decided that she was the one to do it. To save these poor women from being preyed on, becoming his next victim. *Stand up for yourself!*

Two steps into her retreat, she spun on her heel.

“Listen to me, Huber. I don’t care if you *are* the second coming of Beethoven. You’re not better than him. Not by a long shot. No one’s going to remember your name in two years, much less two-hundred. But I’m sure this won’t deter you from going around, telling everyone how wonderful you are. I’m surprised the orchestra was able to fit on the stage, with your inflated ego, you pompous jerk!”

He watched her as she spoke, that smug smile dissolving. His eyes narrowed and what was left in its place was pure, naked humiliation. Professor Marsden had never looked like that. He opened his mouth to speak, and nothing came out. As he fumbled for words, the women around him stared in shock, absolutely silent.

Oh, God. I’ve gone too far. Great job, Diana. He’ll probably commit suicide in his dressing room now.

She thought about apologizing, but this time, the instinct to flee won out. She whirled around, broke through the crowd, and made her exit, before she could say anything else she regretted.

CHAPTER NINE

When Diana reached the bench, the woman who'd fainted was still there, fanning her face with her hand, looking a bit healthier as the security guard fed her a paper cup of water. She said, "Did you get it signed?"

Diana shook her head and handed her the program. "I'm sorry, I couldn't do it."

"What happened?" the woman cried as if she just announced the world was coming to an end.

"Again. I'm sorry." *I just had to withstand a proposition from the Big Head. Who cares about getting him to sign the darn program?* She thought, eyeing the garbage can nearby. She might have thrown her program away, if not for the rest of the orchestra. No, despite Lukas Huber, she wanted to remember this night. But right now, she wanted to create as much distance between herself and that clod as possible. "I've got to go."

She nodded at the two security guards and walked down the narrow hallway, to the exit.

Outside, the rain had stopped. Puddles dotted the ground, the streetlights shining in each one. The night was cool, but clear, and a bit humid. She walked across the street and into a park. Though it was dark, there, there seemed to be a lot of people walking about, many dressed so elegantly that they must've come from the concert, so Diana wasn't worried about her safety. She stepped on the damp green grass, listening to the crickets chirping, and thought of the beautiful music she'd heard.

It'd been a night to remember, definitely. She'd wanted to see a live orchestra, all her life, and so that had happened.

But then . . . she'd gone and ruined it by meeting the ego.

And she still hadn't accomplished anything on her bucket list. She'd wanted to stand up for herself, but instead, she felt like a big clod. There was a difference between standing up for oneself and acting like an idiot. He was a genius, a musical prodigy who was clearly loved all over Austria. Who was she to go in there and tell him about his music?

She stopped at a large statue on a dais in the green, of an elderly Brahms, seated, peering downward, almost as if asleep. On the base of the statue was a female, playing a lyre. Unlike the statue of Johann Strauss, this one didn't have a line for photographs. Of course, it was so dark, she didn't bother to take a selfie, because she doubted it would come out very well.

So instead, Diana stared quietly up at it. *So what do you think, Herr Brahms? Is Lukas Huber God's gift to music?*

Only a slight breeze answered back.

I thought not.

Still, I shouldn't have told him that. Some things are better kept to oneself.

She sighed. She'd heard, from the grapevine, that Professor Marsden had eventually given up teaching. He'd spent his life writing a book on the Civil War that, when published, was panned by critics. After that, he'd been so distraught of his life's work being for nothing, that he simply couldn't stand up in front of a classroom, ever again.

The point was that the most fragile people seemed to hide behind what appeared to be massive egos. Maybe that's all Lukas Huber was—bravado, and nothing else.

And I really did want to get my program signed by Mr. Future Beethoven.

She looked up at Brahms. "What do you think I should do?" she asked aloud. When he didn't answer, she stepped closer. "Hello? I didn't hear you?"

She sighed. The thing was, as much as she wanted to stand up for herself, it didn't mean acting like a total jerk. And she kind of had been one. She knew very little about music, and he was an artist. If some intern had come into her office when she worked at *Addict* cosmetics and told her how to run her marketing department, she'd be just as angry. He'd only been responding to her, acting like an ass in the first place.

So what if he'd propositioned her? *Forgive. Feel the calmness and clarity of letting go.*

Diana checked her watch. It was not yet ten. She could go back to the hotel, take a hot bath, and plan the rest of her sightseeing for tomorrow. *Or,* she could check and see if Lukas Huber was still there.

Not for a roll in the hay, as he'd suggested. Just for an apology. She probably owed him one of those. Yes, he'd been a clod to her, but he'd also been under enormous pressure, and she'd insulted him in what was practically his own house, in front of his many admirers. So in addition to, *Forgive. Feel the calmness and clarity of letting go . . .* she could also make amends.

That would make her feel better.

Yes.

Maybe that would be the only way to feel calm—by clearing her conscience. *Then* maybe she could enjoy the rest of her time in the Music City.

*

She didn't go right back to the music hall. She walked around the park in a circle, thinking. Deciding she couldn't go back to her hotel without at least speaking one more time to Lukas Huber, she turned and quickly headed back across the street to *Musikverein*. When she reached the building, she climbed the steps and went inside. There were only a few well-dressed people lingering about, who'd obviously attended the performance, chatting together. A couple of men with black instrument cases hurried down the stairs. They ignored her as she slipped inside.

The main lobby was empty, except for a janitor who was vacuuming the lush red carpet. He paid no mind to her. She stole across the room and disappeared through the curtain without running into another soul. The hallway to the back was empty, now, as well. As she crept quietly toward where she'd last seen Lukas Huber, she listened for his pompous voice, but heard nothing. When she reached the corner, she peered into the vestibule where she'd last seen him and his many fans.

Now, it was empty. Apparently, they'd all finally stopped fawning over him and gone home. There were no orchestra members around, either; the place had quickly cleared out. Even security was now gone.

She walked into the middle of the vestibule and looked around. There was a set of double doors, which must have led to the stage, a supply closet, and another hallway, stretching even farther to the back of the building.

She took the hallway, scanning the doors. They weren't marked. As she walked, a door suddenly flung open in front of her, and a man came out, carrying a couple of music stands. He jumped back as she did, just as surprised as she was. *"Oida!"* he shouted, patting his chest. *"Was machst du hier?"*

"Sorry, I—" She had to pause to catch the breath that had whooshed out of her lungs from the shock. The man was wearing a headset and jeans, and looked like he must've been part of the crew. "I just came to see if Lukas Huber was still around?"

The corner of his mouth lifted up in a smile as he stared her up and down. She did the same. Probably about ten years older than Diana, he had graying whiskers on his chin and sunken eyes under an almost comically unruly unibrow. He had the gray, wild hair, too, that reminded her of Beethoven—a very popular look among the musically-oriented in Vienna, she realized. "Of course you are."

It was no surprise that Huber was a ladies' man. She hovered there, wondering if she should abandon the mission. After all, there was a good chance, if he was still around, that he was with some other female company. He'd certainly had enough to choose from, when she'd last seen him. Then she looked down at her program. *No, if he's occupied, he just won't answer the door, and that will be that. You can do this.*

"Could you please tell me if he's around?"

The man shrugged. "I saw him go into his dressing room about ten minutes ago. I don't think he's left. He usually stays late." He pointed down the hall. "Third door on your right."

"Thank you," she said, heading that way. When she arrived in front of it, she found the door open about an inch. The sliver of space inside was mostly dark. She listened for a moment, hearing nothing. She raised her hand to knock, then turned to see the crewman staring at her, as if he was interested in seeing what would happen next. When she caught his eye, he quickly turned and headed off.

Once he was gone, she rapped lightly on the door and waited.

No answer.

She lifted her knuckles to the door and rapped again, a little louder.

Still, no answer. *Maybe the crewman's mistaken and he's already left. Or maybe he is in there with someone and doesn't want to be disturbed.*

She took a step away, thinking. *If he's not in there, then why did he leave the door open?*

Diana decided to try one more time. She knocked once more, and called, "Mr. Huber?" This time, her knock was hard enough to nudge the door open slightly. One more nudge, and she was able to stick her head through.

The dressing room was dark. There was only a small, dull light, illuminating a vanity mirror filled with photographs and programs belonging to the great pianist. Other than that, she could barely see anything.

So he did go home, Diana thought, disappointed.

She went to leave, but then she noticed a neat stack of press photographs sitting on the vanity. They were small, the size of a bookmark, but Diana could see his dark hair, and the scrawl of his signature over the face.

Oh, I'm sure he won't mind if I grab one of those, she thought, pushing the door open a little more. *That's what he signed them for.*

But as she pushed the door open, it shoved up against something, and would not go farther. She shoved again, and whatever was behind it gave way slightly, allowing her to move into the room. She reached forward, grabbed the press photo, and smiled at it. He certainly *was* handsome. And clearly talented. She couldn't blame women for going gaga over him, even if he was a bit of a blowhard.

I'll take two, just in case, she thought, grabbing another one. *He won't miss them.*

She tucked them into her evening bag.

I guess I'll have to save my apology, she thought, turning to leave. *I doubt I'll ever see him again, now. I guess I'll just have to go home and plan the rest of my trip.*

As she spun, she stepped on someone's foot. So hard, she heard the bones cracking and the skin shifting under her foot. She cringed. *That had to have hurt.*

Luckily, no one complained.

"Oh, I'm sorry," she mumbled carelessly, tripping off of it and grabbing hold of the door.

Suddenly, the weight of what she'd done hit her, and she froze.

Right in front of her, there was a light switch. Bracing herself, she reached over and flipped it on.

Light flooded the room, and she scanned to the floor, already having an idea of what she might see.

No, she hadn't stepped on a foot. It was a hand. A bare, cupped hand, palm upwards.

There, sprawled on his stomach, was a small man with long, dark hair. Lukas Huber.

Heart beating fast, she bent down and looked closer. "Lukas Huber?" she asked, daring to reach forward and nudge back one of those long, flowing locks of hair that had fallen into his face. "Are you okay?"

No, he clearly wasn't okay. His eyes were wide open, bulging and staring emptily, the skin of his cheek was a bright purple, his tongue was lolling from his half-open mouth, and he wasn't moving at all.

By now, Diana had seen enough of this to know for sure. Lukas Huber wasn't going to be okay, any time soon.

He was certainly dead.

But though she'd seen all this before, that didn't stop her from rushing away, screaming.

CHAPTER TEN

"What is the problem?" the hairy crewman she'd seen earlier said, intercepting her at the end of the hall.

"D-d-dead," she managed, pointing behind her. "Lukas Huber is dead."

"Dead?" He gave her a doubtful look. "Are you sure?"

She nodded, feeling faint. She swooned against a wall, gripping it for dear life, just like Huber's fan had done, not thirty minutes earlier, in that very spot.

"Where?"

"In his dressing room. On the f-f-floor."

He started to move that way, then looked back at her, waiting for her to accompany him, but she shook her head. She thought of his bloated purple face and bug-eyes and her stomach felt weak; she didn't want to see that sight, ever again.

He motioned her forward. "Show me."

She hesitated. "Shouldn't we call 9-1-1, or whatever it is you have here?"

"Not yet. I need to see."

Of course, he didn't believe her. Why would he? Only an hour before, Lukas Huber had been lecturing those many admirers, in the prime of his life. Without seeing it, it seemed impossible that such a force could no longer be among the living. She didn't even believe it, when she'd said the words aloud.

But she had *seen* it. And she really wished, right now, that she could unsee it.

Fine. I'll take him to the door, but I'm not going in.

She led him to the dressing room door and pointed, planting her feet and doing her best to squeeze her eyes closed. It didn't work. The crewman made a gagging noise, and the second she opened her eyes to make sure he was all right, through the crack in the door, she could see his hand, curled a bit, like it had been clutching at something. Fighting . . . against someone.

Oh, God. Was this a murder?

Another murder?

The crewman went in and bent over the body. Shoved it over and looked closely at it. "*Krass. Die Oaschkortn ziagn.*"

"What?" she asked, confused. "Should you be touching the body like—"

"Looks like he's dead, for sure. Not all that long ago either, because his skin is still warm," he said, sounding more amused than worried. "Strangled with his cravat."

Oh, no. "Strangled?"

"That's what it looks like," he said, shoving the body over again like it was a hunk of meat. She didn't know much about police procedurals, but that definitely didn't seem like a good move. She wondered briefly if it would come back to haunt her.

"But who could've done it? I was just here, not an hour ago."

He looked around. "Don't know. Looks like someone must've just come up from behind him and surprised him while he was sitting at his vanity. You were with him before, with all his admirers. And just now . . . so I think you'd know better than I do."

Diana's insides jumped. *Great. So he thinks I did it?* Funny, though she'd been down this road before, being accused for something she didn't do, it was no easier, the third time around. In fact, now, she was even more nervous, because she'd been through it all before. Didn't that make her suspicious? "Yes, but—"

"I just clean up after him and all his messes. He's never even talked to me. I'm not pretty enough, I guess." He grinned and reached into the pocket of his trousers for his phone. When he jabbed in a number, he started to speak rapidly in German, but the one word Diana did understand, *Polizei,* led her to understand that he was finally calling the police. When he hung up, he said, "They'll be right over. Well, all that lady-killing's finally caught up with him, I'd say. One of them killed him."

"You think?"

He shrugged. "What other explanation do you have?"

She saw what he meant. The other two murders she'd discovered, there'd been some doubt as to the cause of death. The first, in Versailles, could've been an accidental fall, and the second, in the dressing room in Verona, Diana thought could've been a heart attack. This time, there was no doubt. People usually didn't go around accidentally strangling themselves with their neck ties.

Three murders in a row. What is the opposite of serendipity? Because that's what I'm cursed with.

She fanned her face, trying to catch her breath. "This—this is a great loss to the music world, I'm sure."

The man snorted and checked his watch. Clearly, he wasn't much of a fan. "Great loss to me, too. I was going to be off the clock in fifteen minutes. Now I guess I got to stick around."

*

Sitting alone in a small rehearsal room of the *Musikverein*, among the music stands and scattered chairs, Diana checked her phone. Ten-forty-five. She'd been sequestered here for a half-hour, with no idea of what was going on.

All of the orchestra had left, as had all of the admirers who'd fawned over Huber and the security guards, so the only people that came to the scene were a few police officers, a couple members of the clean-up crew, and Diana. The police had immediately arrived and ushered her here, telling her to wait.

But for how long?

She pulled out her phone and turned it off silent mode. Immediately, a number of messages showed up. One from Bea: *I think I'm going to have a separate reception in the States so that friends can come.* One from Lily: *Mom, look at the nightmare that's outside the house!* with a picture of a horrible pink unicorn sculpture the renters had put outside the Long Island home she'd lived in for thirty years, right in front of Diana's favorite hydrangea bushes. And one from Evan: *I'm confused—so you're not back in the States?*

She groaned aloud, and typed in: *FOR THE LAST TIME, I AM IN AUSTRIA.*

Just then, the door opened, and a large man with a boxy frame walked in. He had a definite Arnold Schwarzeneggar look to him—one that said, *Don't mess with me.* His dress shirt stretched precariously around the muscles of his biceps and chest, threatening to tear with any wrong move, Incredible Hulk-style, and he had to duck so his head wouldn't hit the transom. His face was just as emotionless and scary as The Terminator's, too, all severe angles and points, from his jawline to his chin, to the tip of his nose, so her first thought was, *I wouldn't want to be on his bad side.*

Then she remembered that she was probably a suspect, and was *already* on his bad side.

He pulled out the chair next to her and sat down. It was like an adult sitting on a child's chair in Kindergarten class—it practically disappeared under his substantial body, and creaked a bit in protest.

"*Frau* St. James?" he said, not looking up from his notepad.

She nodded. "Yes. That's me."

"I'm Detective Josef Moser, from the Vienna Police." When he did look up at her, she withered a bit. His blue eyes were serious, icy enough to pierce right through her chest. *You are terminated.* "You are American, from what I hear?"

He said it like it wasn't a good thing. Would he count that against her? "Uh, yes."

"What brings you to Vienna? Vacation?"

"Well, sort of. I was travelling through Europe for a year. This is my third stop on my tour."

"You arrived today? From . . ."

"Yes. From Verona, Italy. I took the train."

"You went to the performance tonight, then?"

She nodded. "Yes, I did. I—"

"Alone?"

She rolled her eyes to the ceiling. *Do you see anyone else with me?* "Yes."

"Fortunate for you, you were able to get a ticket. How did that come about? It's not very easy to get a seat here in *Musikverein*, from what I hear."

"Yes. I stopped by *Theater an de Wien* and inquired after a ticket. And they told me they'd contact me if anything became available. And one did. So I guess I was lucky that happened." *Or unlucky, now that I think about it . . .*

"All right. Can you walk me through what happened?"

She nodded. "Like I said, I went to the performance earlier tonight and thought the soloist was very good. I wanted to tell him how good and perhaps get my program signed. So I went into the back of the theater, and that gentleman from the crew, the one who called you, pointed out his dressing room to me." She felt her heart speed up in her chest as she recounted the next moments. "Anyway, the door was slightly open. I didn't see him at first, because it was dark. I thought he wasn't there, but I noticed some signed photographs on his vanity. I went to get one, and that's when I noticed him. So I ran out and told the first person I saw—the crewman."

"Mr. Gruber," he offered.

"Okay."

"Hmm." He looked down at his notes. "You didn't touch the body?"

"No. Well . . . I moved his hair away from his face. And I . . ." Her face heated. "I stepped on his hand when I was going in."

"Ah. That explains the heel-mark on his palm."

She gritted her teeth. "Yes. Um. Sorry about that. The crewman—Mr. Gruber, I guess—he moved the body. He turned it over to see if he was breathing. I wasn't sure if he should, but before I could--"

"And that's all?" He stared at her expectantly, as if wanting her to say more.

Was there any more? She shook her head. "Well . . . yes, that about sums it up."

"You didn't have any other interaction with Herr Huber, prior to his demise?"

"No . . ." Was he fishing for something? She withered some more as those blue eyes connected with hers. He seemed exasperated about something she'd said, bordering on angry. *You wouldn't like me when I'm angry.*

His eyebrows tented. "Mr. Gruber says you were in the back of *Musikverein* before that, and that you were one of the last people to see him alive?"

She blinked. Right. She'd forgotten about that. "Yes. I did go there, prior, but then I left before getting his signature."

"You left?" He looked doubtful. "Why?"

She paused. Should she tell him about the tense exchange she'd had with Huber? Did it matter? Wouldn't that just put a target on her back? Thinking quickly, she decided to fudge it: "I don't know. He was very busy with many of his female admirers. And I guess I got cold feet, waiting for it. I decided to go back because . . . well, I decided I really wanted it."

Moser started to go through his notes, and his phone buzzed. He picked it up. "*Ja*?" he spoke into it, sounding angry.

So it wasn't just her. He was angry with everyone. She relaxed a little as he listened to the person on the other end.

Just then, her phone buzzed with a text. She took her phone out and glanced at it. It was her ex-husband. *No need to shout. Then what is this bunk about the Music City? Are you trying to confuse me, Love?*

She gnashed her teeth. *Cultured* was never a word she'd use to describe Evan.

She quickly typed in, *I'm in Vienna. Austria. Vienna is ALSO called the Music City, Evan. In fact, it is the FIRST Music City, believe it or not.* She thought about typing in, *You narrow-minded fool. How did we ever stay married for nearly three decades? Go listen to Tilda's pop-favorites playlist and leave me alone,* but she'd decided she'd made her point.

As she was typing, the detective ended his call and cleared his throat loudly. She looked up as he said, "Mr. Gruber said that you had some kind of confrontation with the victim?"

Diana's heart stopped. Had Mr. Gruber seen *everything* that happened? What was he, like the all-seeing-eye of *Musikverein*? And if so, why hadn't she noticed *him* at all? It had been crowded there, but she'd have noticed a man among the sea of women, fawning over Huber, wouldn't she? "No, not a confrontation, exactly."

The officer flipped back a few pages on his notebook. "It says here that you told Herr Huber, *I'm surprised the orchestra was able to fit on the stage, with your inflated ego, you pompous jerk!*" He raised an eyebrow for confirmation. "What is that, if not a confrontation, *Frau* St. James?"

Yes, she had said that, word for word. Mr. Gruber had a remarkably good memory. "Yes, I had. Because he'd said some pretty vile things to me, propositioned me, and—"

"And you . . ." He asked her another question, which she didn't hear, because just as he was in the midst of it, her phone buzzed with another text from Evan. *Wow. That's interesting. Never realized it. Tilda might like to see that. She likes music. Where are you staying?*

Diana stared at it. Heck, no. If she told him that, they might show up on the next flight. That's what had happened at Verona. Tilda and Evan had wound up following her through Italy because she liked that "Shakespeare guy." Diana could just imagine how she'd be with classical music. She probably thought Handel was a department store.

"Hmm?" she asked, as she looked up and realized the officer was staring at her, waiting for an answer. "I'm sorry. My ex is a bit n—"

He gave her a look that said he didn't care, freezing her vocal cords.

And she really didn't want to talk about Evan, anyway. "Could you repeat yourself? I missed that question."

He looked up at the ceiling before settling those piercing blue eyes on her. "I asked, if you went back to the music hall, hoping to take him up on that offer."

Offer. Her mind had gone blank of everything except the vision of Tilda, clapping and wolf-whistling with wild abandon in between movements of a symphony, while the rest of the hall stared at her in disgust. Or even worse, falling asleep and snoring. Not that Diana had been much better, with her cell phone faux pas. "I'm sorry. What offer?"

The officer looked irritated, now. She quickly pocketed her phone; thanks to Evan, she was treading on thin ice with the Terminator. "The proposition you referred to? I'm assuming, for sexual--"

"Certainly not!" she cried in indignation. "What? No! Look, he was a chauvinistic pig. And he did have a huge ego, comparing himself to Beethoven. That much was obvious. But I had no reason to kill him. I just felt guilty about the exchange, wanted to apologize, and hoped I could get the program signed. That's the only reason I went back."

He tapped a pen to his paper. "I find it very peculiar that if that's all you wanted, you wouldn't have just gotten that the first time. What stopped you the first time, and why come back?"

She sighed. "Because, like I said, he propositioned me. I was flustered and embarrassed. But then I went and talked to Brahms, and I realized I really wanted his signature, even if he was a pig. So I was going to apologize, smooth things over, and see if I could get the signature, since this is a once in a lifetime trip and I didn't want to regret it, later . . ."

"Who is this Brahms? Can he corroborate your story?"

She squinted at him. "No, he's dead."

"Dead?" His eyes shot to hers in alarm. "What happened to him?"

"The statue."

"You talked to a statue?"

She nodded. "Brahms, the composer. In the park across the street. You . . . don't follow classical music?"

He shook his head. "I'm not a fan. Why were you talking to a statue? Did it talk back? Are you saying it told you to come back here? Like . . . voices in your head? Are you under medical care?"

Oh my God. I sound like a lunatic. I can just imagine the headline: Woman claims she murdered legendary musician Lukas Huber because the ghost of Brahms told her to do it. "No. Forget the statue. I just went for a walk in the park and had a change of heart. That's all."

"Hmm," he said again. "A couple of the security guards said that you left after the confrontation, and seemed rather flustered. So this was after he propositioned you?"

She nodded miserably. "Yes! Right. He'd just asked me to meet him out back for a little fun. So I told him off. And then I left abruptly. But I came back when I had that change of heart. You see, I have this itinerary, and one of the things on it is to fo--"

"You came back after you talked to this Brahms."

She'd been going through her evening bag for her itinerary, but she let out a groan. "The statue. Yes."

"And yet, as much as you disliked the man, you still wanted Huber to sign your program."

She sighed. *A fact I'm regretting more and more by the minute.* "He is—uh, *was*—the Next Beethoven, after all." She pulled out her itinerary and showed it to him. "See? *Forgive. Feel the calmness and clarity of letting go.* That's what I was trying to do."

Moser glanced at it with little interest, then fell silent, checking his notes. The thought suddenly struck her. Lukas Huber was dead. His career was over. His body of work would never be added to. Like a young Franz Schubert, he'd been cut off in his prime. He may have been a jerk, but he didn't deserve death. And who knew what beautiful, yet-to-be-created masterpieces the world would lose out on, with his flame extinguished?

Her heart twisted. As it did, her phone buzzed again in her pocket. This time, she didn't bother looking at it.

"I can't possibly be a suspect. I was seen leaving, and coming back. And Mr. Gruber saw me go in the second time. There couldn't be enough time for me to have killed him. Right?" she asked hopefully.

He didn't look at her. "We're ruling nothing and no one out. All we know is that security was rather lax; there are no cameras in the vicinity, so it's going to make our job all the more difficult. Apparently, this Huber fellow had some very well-connected friends, and I can guarantee we'll be placing a lot of our manpower into finding the killer. Where are you staying, Frau St. James?"

"The Hotel Beethoven," she answered, knowing exactly what he'd say next. *Don't go anywhere. We'll be in touch.*

"All right," he said, standing up and handing her a business card. "Thanks for the information. We may be in touch with you, but if you have anything at all, please contact me. You may go, but please don't leave the city until we've gotten this sorted out. All right?"

Perfectly. What he meant to say was, *I'll be back.* Likely, with her luck, again and again and again, until she was sick of him.

Or until he'd pigeon-holed her as the murderer.

She nodded and stood, then took out her phone. The first thing that greeted her was the text from Evan: *I sent Tillie a link to Austria—she says it looks great! How are the beaches there? Let's talk.*

Her stomach roiled.

Now, it was after eleven. She was tired. She was hungry, since she hadn't eaten much, thanks to Hans. But most of all, she was frustrated. She'd been through this drill before, and both times before, she'd been subjected to endless questioning and suspicion from the local police, so much of it that her tour of the area had been anything but typical. Was that going to happen again? If so, she didn't know if she could take it.

"It's this dress," she whined half-coherently as she meandered, toward the door. "I think it's bad luck. This is the second time I've worn it, and someone has been murdered."

The officer tilted his head. "What? What did you say?"

She whimpered miserably. "Someone was murdered when I was in Verona. Of course, the killer was caught. The killer was caught for the murder I witnessed in Paris, too. I helped."

"Are you saying you witnessed three murders? When were these?"

"Oh. A few weeks ago," she murmured absently, then took notice of the officer's interest. Was this going to get her in trouble? Probably. How many people witnessed a murder in their lifetime, much less three, in one summer?

Suddenly, she stiffened. This was *definitely* going to get her in trouble. *Oh, no, what have I done?*

She quickly added, "They caught the killers, though. And in neither case, was it me."

That didn't seem to faze him. He wrote something on his pad and underlined it several times. She couldn't help thinking it was the word, GUILTY. "Just . . . stick around, Frau St. James. I am sure we'll have more questions for you."

I'm sure you will, too, she thought as she headed outside, to go back to her hotel and try to sleep off the memory of this hellish night. *Moved to tears by beautiful music?*

She felt near tears, but there was no music at all to be heard, even in the city known for it. Outside, in the cool air of near midnight, there was no sound at all. Nothing. And all she knew for sure was one thing—They were going to make the rest of her time in Austria just like her time in France and Italy—full of twists and turns.

CHAPTER ELEVEN

Diana was so exhausted that she decided to take a taxi from *Musikverein*, even though it was a pleasant walk away from the hotel. An eerie mist shrouded the city, hovering over the shoulders like cloaks of the many statues of the renowned, making her shiver for lack of one. As the taxi whisked her away into the foggy night, she yawned and glanced at her phone.

It'd blown up. Lily was still searching for her earrings, and was now wondering if she might have left them on the plane. Bea was still trying to plan the wedding of the century. And Evan wanted her tips for his next vacation with Tilda. Sure, at eleven in the evening in Austria, it was right around dinnertime in New York, but that didn't mean they could pepper her with all their troubles and problems. Couldn't they handle anything themselves?

Groaning, she decided not to answer a single one of their inquiries. It could wait until tomorrow, when she was feeling less tired. Less anxious. And when she didn't have a massive headache pounding at both sides of her head.

Ow, she thought, touching her temple. It had crept up on her, the migraine, and was a direct result of Lukas Huber's murder. After all, the music had been so beautiful and calming—it was everything that happened afterwards that had made the evening go downhill.

The cab pulled up in front of the hotel. As she paid the driver and stepped out, it'd begun to rain again. She slammed the door hard, and started to walk, only stopping when she felt a tug behind her and heard the unmistakable sound of fabric ripping. She glanced over her shoulder just in time to see the chiffon material of her dress hem caught in the door of the taxi, waving cheerfully, like a flag, in its wake.

It drove away, taking a large part of the back of her dress with her.

"Oh!" she shouted, as one of the valets came running to her assistance. Cool air rushed against the back of her legs, and she reached behind her, afraid of what she might find.

Sure enough, her beautiful dress had become a mini-dress. A *very* mini dress. Luckily, it seemed to cover her parts, and she was still decent, but her dress had definitely seen better days.

"*Kann ich Ihnen helfen?*" the valet said to her.

She didn't know what that meant. All she knew was that she was very close to tears, and it had nothing to do with music.

"Doesn't matter," she said with a laugh. "I was planning on burning this dress, anyway. It's unlucky."

He gave her a questioning look as he opened the door for her. *"Gute Nacht, Frau."*

"Danke schön."

She went inside and scrubbed a hand down her face when she got into the elevator. As it climbed, she looked at herself in the mirrored doors. She looked old and exhausted, a mere shade of the excited woman who'd entered this elevator, only hours before.

She went to her room, still playing over the events of the night. The nightmare meeting with Hans, that actually seemed quite pleasant now, compared to *other* things that had happened. The beautiful music. The encounter with Lukas. Yelling at him. And of course, finding his strangled body on the floor of the dressing room.

She shuddered as she tossed her ruined dress in the garbage can and climbed into bed. *Just go to sleep. Things will look better in the morning.*

She didn't really believe that, but she told herself that little lie, again and again, until eventually, she managed to drift off.

*

Diana was sitting in her seat in the crowded *Musikverein*, waiting for the show to begin. For some reason, though, she was in the very front, away from the rest of the audience. In fact, she was nearly on the stage herself, as one of the performers. As before, the conductor came out, and everyone applauded. He stepped aside and began to applaud, too, as Lukas Huber appeared, smiling that dashing, confident smile of his.

Lukas lifted his tails, stepped to the piano, sat down and started to play. But this time, he wasn't playing the classical music he'd played the previous night. No, he was playing *The Entertainer,* and it sounded just like the flat notes, coming from her ringtone. Diana looked around to see if anyone was confused, but the audience was absolutely rapt by the simple performance.

As he played, the members of the orchestra, behind him, began to dance, spinning around and putting their hands up in the air as if they were at some rock concert. Eventually, the audience began to clap along with the song, as they often did in the PBS New Year's Concert, when a particularly lively waltz was being performed.

As the music swelled through the renowned music hall, the concertmaster set down his violin and walked behind Huber, smiling from ear to ear. Huber continued to play, even as the concertmaster reached around his neck and untied his cravat. In fact, he seemed thrilled by it, still grinning, as the music began to speed up.

In the audience, people began to clap faster.

The concertmaster wound the ends of the cravat around his hands, and Diana knew what was happening. But she was glued to her seat. She tried to say something in protest, but her heart flew into her throat.

Then, suddenly, the concertmaster reached over with the garrote and started to strangle Huber. He flew backwards, the top of his head resting against the concertmaster's chest as the life was squeezed out of him, but even so, his hands did not miss a note. No, in fact, he began to play faster.

People clapped even harder. The orchestra members began to spin even faster, until they were a blur.

Diana finally ripped herself from her seat, and as she did, the entire back of her dress came off. People began to laugh at her, but no one seemed to notice that Lukas Huber was being murdered, on stage. She pointed, screamed, and shouted, and yet everyone just laughed at her, and clapped along to the music.

She turned in horror to see Huber, still playing, his eyes bulging and his tongue protruding from his purple lips. He was still smiling.

Then, she turned back to the audience, only to find that every single seat was occupied by a Hans. There were hundreds of baskets of wiener schnitzel, and he had his napkin around his collar, gorging on them. Diana tried to climb up onto the stage, but realized she was wading in a sea of wiener schnitzel, up to her waist, so much of it she couldn't move. "Hans!" she cried. "Hans! Help him. He's dying!"

Hans merely laughed, chunks of chewed-up food sputtering from his fat lips, and said, "You're nothing but a crook!"

And he pointed at her.

As he did, the police arrived. Officer Josef Moser parted the piles of wiener schnitzel like the Red Sea, handcuffs ready to snap onto her wrists . . .

She jumped up in bed, heart pounding, and looked around. The morning sun was slashing through the blinds, and birds were singing cheerily outdoors.

A dream. Nothing but a crazy dream.

Diana threw her head back against the headboard, strange, disjointed bits of the dream still floating through her mind, and sighed. *Well, it's morning, and things are supposed to be better. How are they better?*

She really couldn't think of anything other than that dream. Grabbing the remote control, she turned on the television, flipping to an English-language news channel. The first thing she saw was a still picture of Lukas Huber, sitting on a piano bench. On the ticker underneath, it said, *RENOWNED PIANIST MURDERED!* A pretty, grave-faced reporter said, "Sad and incredibly shocking news today from *Musikverein.* It appears the celebrated pianist Lukas Huber was murdered last night, as he was preparing to leave the venue. No suspect has been named and the police are still investigating. Huber was a noted composer who'd last night performed his new Jupiter Symphony to a sold-out crowd . . ."

Diana turned off the television.

No, things weren't better. Not at all.

She sat up in bed and called room service, ordering what was listed, on the menu, the Viennese Deluxe Breakfast, which included bread rolls, jam, a boiled egg, ham and cheese, and a mélange, Austria's version of frothed milk and steamed coffee. *Maybe a full stomach will make me feel better. And I'll eat room service because there'll be no chance of Hans dropping in on my meal.*

As she went to turn on the water for the shower, the phone to her hotel room started to ring. She rushed to grab it. "Hello?"

"*Guten Tag, Frau* St. James," a voice said, which she instantly recognized as the cop from last night. "This is Josef Moser."

"Oh. Hello."

"I wanted to make sure we had the right location for you."

"Well, you found me," she said. *Even if you haven't found Huber's killer, yet.* "Good job."

"Yes." He didn't seem amused. In fact, his voice sounded distinctly, well, angry, just like he looked. "Can I bother you for a moment?"

"Uh. Yes. Sure." She took a deep breath. "What can I help you with, officer?"

"Well, I'm just trying to get the timelines straight. What time do you think you left the music hall, the first time, after interacting with the victim?"

She hadn't checked, but last night, in bed, she'd put together her timeline, so she could answer these questions easily. It helped to have gone through this kind of thing before; she knew exactly what the officers were going to want to know. "The concert ended at around nine-fifteen. I remember that because I did look at my phone. So probably about nine-thirty, nine-forty?"

"And you returned . . . ?"

"I was only outside for a few minutes. Actually, maybe more like fifteen, twenty. I checked my watch before I went back. It was about five of ten."

She hoped that information, as clear as she'd made it, would get her off the hook. After all, at what point did they think she'd committed this murder? The first time, when she was surrounded by his admirers, or the second time, when she'd only been there for a period of no more than three minutes? Plus, there was the matter of—how could any woman be strong enough to strangle a man, even a smaller one? She wouldn't even know where to start with that. Wouldn't *want* to know.

Instead, he simply said, "Hmm. Thank you. We'll be in touch."

And then the line went dead.

Great. *Nice talking to you, too, Detective. Have a great day.*

She hopped into the shower, thinking about Lukas Huber. Sure, the police were probably way ahead of her. But every moment they spent concentrating on Diana as a suspect was one moment that took away from focusing on the *real* killer.

But who could that be?

Diana's mind automatically went to the rabid fans that had been crowding around Lukas Huber after the concert. Many of them hadn't seemed quite right in the head, with the way they were excessively fawning over the man. Maybe it had been a fan with a couple of screws loose, who'd taken her love for the pianist a bit too far.

That was probably a safe bet.

But then again, a woman, murdering a man in that way? Huber was a slight man, but it would have had to be a woman with a considerable amount of strength.

Or, who knew? Maybe there was someone on the orchestra who was jealous of Huber, for having the talent that they didn't have to be a soloist. Not to mention that Huber had a personality that probably rubbed many the wrong way. In fact, it could've been anybody who'd been in the building in the time between when she'd left him with that crowd, and when she returned. Considering security hadn't seemed very on top of things, last night, anyone could have sneaked into the back area, there. Maybe someone was lying in wait, in his dressing room, just anticipating his return?

But *who*?

As Diana finished her shower and stepped out, someone knocked on the door. Her room service. She twisted her hair into a towel and threw on the hotel-provided robe, then rushed for the door. The smell of cooked ham, fresh bread, and coffee made her mouth water as the tray was wheeled in.

"Thank you," she said, signing her check on the billfold and handing it to the man. "It looks lovely."

He bowed and left, and she pounced on the food, slathering strawberry jam on a piece of warm, fresh bread. She took a bite and let out a moan of delight. It was so good, her stomach thanked her.

"It's got to be one of his fans," she said aloud. She polished off the bread and licked the jam from her fingers. "Guaranteed. They were a few sandwiches short of a picnic."

She made a mental list of the women who'd been there. There'd been the lady with her son. It seemed pretty safe to knock them off the suspect list, since she was with her son, after all, and Diana had watched them leave. Plus, the lady was small, frail. No way could she have done something like garrote a man.

Then there was the woman who'd fainted. Well, she was certainly larger, but she likely wouldn't have had the strength. She was older, too. No, she didn't seem like a likely suspect, either.

Diana closed her eyes and tried to remember the other people who'd been there. The security guards were a possibility. And of course, Mr. Gruber could've done it, too.

But her thoughts kept going to the many fans, just because they'd been so, well, fanatical.

Suddenly, her mind fastened on the woman who'd been standing very close to Huber while he spoke, almost at his elbow. She'd been so gorgeous, it was hard not to notice her, even in a sea of people. Her bare shoulders were muscular, the sign of someone who was fit and strong enough to murder a small-statured man like Huber. She'd had that dark, wild ebony hair, so beautiful and shiny that Diana had noticed it while sitting in the concert hall, waiting for the music to begin. She'd been sitting a couple rows ahead of Diana.

Diana lowered herself down onto the edge of the bed.

Of course.

The concert halls kept record of everyone who bought a ticket, didn't they? If she could get back to *Musikverein,* and somehow go through the list of people who'd gotten tickets for the performance, based on the general location of the seat, she might be able to find out the woman's name.

That was someone the police probably weren't looking into. When Diana had gone back, the second time, the woman was nowhere to be found. They likely didn't even know she'd been there.

But Diana did.

I should probably call the officer and tell him what I know, and stay out of it. Yes, that would be the smart thing.

She grabbed her phone and found the card for Josef Moser, then dialed the number. He answered at once. "Moser."

"Hi. Detective Moser. This is—"

"*Frau* St. James. What can I do for you?" His voice was slightly nicer than a bark.

"I was just thinking of last night, and some possible people that might have done it," she said. "There was a woman who was sitting a few rows ahead of me. I noticed her because of her dark hair, and she was also backstage after the—"

"We're already contacting all the people who were at the concert. But thank you. We've got it under control," he said, in a tone that said, *Stay in your lane.*

"Well, you had asked me to call if I remembered anything, and—"

"Yes. Thank you for the help. But right now, we're on it. If you remember anything other than people we're already looking into, feel free to call."

"Oh." *So basically, when you said, "Call me if you remember anything," you meant, "Call me if you want to confess?"* "All right. Have a good day."

She hung up, feeling silly. The police didn't want her help. They just wanted to catch her in a lie. Was that it?

"Fine," she muttered under her breath. "I'll stay out of it."

But then, she smiled. *Or maybe I could just look into it myself.*

That, she was sure, would bring her closer to the killer. Plus, if she did that, then she could be absolutely sure that *something* was being done that wasn't focused on her as the main suspect.

Diana finished polishing off her breakfast, grabbed her bag and phone, and stepped out the door, heading back to *Musikverein.*

CHAPTER TWELVE

It was a gorgeous mid-summer day, the sun shining brightly among the many trees and historic buildings, the cloudless blue sky overhead, not a threat of rain anywhere. A perfect day for sightseeing. But as she hurried down the street, past the statues and memorials for various important Austrian figures, Diana had something else on her mind.

Murder.

She reached the building and gazed up at it. In the full sunlight, she could admire more fully the Neoclassical architecture. It was red plaster, with ionic columns in the front, and several statues above the door and on the roof. Even in her haste, she couldn't help gazing at it in wonder. She imagined all of the historical figures who had once graced the halls over the centuries, and wondered what other secrets it held. Its walls knew who had murdered Lukas Huber. Had anyone else ever been murdered there?

She shuddered a little at the thought.

Then she followed the signs around the corner, to the box office, hoping it wasn't too early. As she arrived there, she noticed two police cruisers, parked at the curb, and two officers stationed near the back entrance to the theater. Her skin prickled with goosebumps as she kept her head down and quickly stepped into the vestibule for the box office.

There were two young people inside the box office, talking in low voices. They seemed so intent on whatever they were talking about that they didn't notice when Diana appeared in the window. She listened to them, trying to make out the words, but she realized they were speaking in German.

She cleared her throat.

One of them, a pretty young girl, turned to her and started to speak in German. She seemed angry, but then again, German *always* sounded angry to Diana.

"I'm sorry. I don't understand."

The girl rolled her eyes. "No ticket sales today. In case you haven't seen it on the news, there's been a bereavement. Lukas Huber, the pianist, was murdered."

She seemed to take great delight in imparting that bit of gossip, but then she sighed in disappointment when Diana's expression didn't give off the shock she was clearly hoping for. She went to pull a shade closed, when the other one in the box said, "Hey. Wait."

Diana squinted to look behind the glass, into the shade of the box to get a better look at the other person. It was the kind young usher who'd showed her to her seat, last night. Diana relaxed. Maybe he'd help her, and her mission wouldn't be so hard.

"Hello," he said, sounding less enthused than he had last night. "I know you."

She smiled. "Yes. I was at the performance last night."

His face turned grave. "Oh, then you've heard. The police said they were going to contact everyone."

The girl laughed. "Dieter, you *Dummkopf.* Everyone's heard. I told you, it was on the news this morning."

Diana nodded. She didn't really want to go into the fact that she'd been the one to find the body. "It's a shock, I'm sure, for everyone."

The girl snorted. "The only shock is that it didn't happen sooner."

The boy laughed. "That's the truth." He looked at Diana and shrugged. "The guy was a bit of an . . . *arschgeige.*"

"A what?"

He shook his head and laughed. "Never mind. He knew how to push people's buttons, that was for sure. Let's just say he didn't have a lot of friends around these parts."

"I heard he was a bit arrogant," Diana offered.

"That's an understatement," the kid scoffed. "I'm not denying he was a great pianist. You obviously saw his talent. Even if he was a little . . . boring."

"Boring?" Diana was confused.

The girl laughed. "A lot of women would beg to differ on that."

He shrugged. "*Silly* women, who don't know a movement in classical music from a bowel movement. He was too technical for my taste. No emotion at all. And as a composer, he was a *Blödmannsgehilfenanwärter*. A complete fraud."

Diana's jaw dropped. That was news to her. "A fraud? Really?"

"There were about a dozen other composers who have accused him of stealing their work. But he gets all the notoriety. There are people around him—mostly women—who love him so much and think he can do no wrong."

The girl smiled. “He is—*was*—really *gutaussehend,* Dieter.”

“Yeah, yeah . . .” The boy rolled his eyes. “Whatever, Sheila. So what if he’s good looking? He was still a sneaky piece of trash, hoping no one would catch on to his little ruse.”

Sheila giggled. “Oh, and you did! You’re so smart, Dieter. Go tell the board of the Philharmonic and see what they say.”

His lips twisted. “I did. And they—”

“They laughed you out of the room. I know. You’d better stop that, if you still want to have a job here. Huber had some powerful friends. They can make it hard on you!”

Diana carefully looked around. “Maybe you can help me?” she started, trying to circle him back to the reason she was there.

Dieter moved forward. “Oh. Right. What can I do for you? You’re not here for tickets?”

“No . . .” she said, quickly cycling through excuses. Why else would she return? Oh, of course. She’d pulled something similar to gain access to Versailles, when she was in Paris. “I left my stole here last night.”

“Stole?”

“Yes. Like a wrap,” she said, motioning with her hands as if she was pulling something tight around her shoulders. “Is it possible I can—”

“Sure, sure. Lost and found is right here,” he said, bending slightly to look at something at his feet. “I don’t think we got anything new since last performance, though. Hold on, I’ll let you in and you can go through it.”

He disappeared for a moment, and a bit later, the lock on the door beside the box office opened and he ducked his head out, motioning her toward him. She quickly followed him inside. When she got into the cramped space, the girl grabbed her keys. “It’s a little tight in here. I’m going to take my morning smoke break. Okay, Dieter?”

Good, Diana thought as she scanned the small office. Other than a cardboard box of left-behind items, there was nothing more than a desk with a computer on it. The information she was looking for was probably in there, and she wouldn’t be able to get it herself. *It’ll make this easier if the girl’s gone.*

Diana stooped and started to go through the stuff, her mind churning. Meanwhile, the kid hovered behind her, gnawing on a fingernail. She knew that he was there because she looked over her shoulder, several times, to find him watching her and chewing noisily. She rifled through the box of things—mittens, a scarf, a billfold, even a single lost shoe-- and let out a dramatic sigh. "Not here!"

He bent down to shove the box under the desk. "Sorry."

Think fast, Diana. If you have to leave this place empty-handed, you're never going to get the information you need. Quick. Make a scene!

"Oh!" She cried, covering her face with her hands. "This is *awful.*"

The kid looked at her like, *Get a grip.*

"It was my mother's you see. And the last thing she ever gave me before she passed," she said, conjuring up some fake tears to go along with it. "And the strangest thing is, I know exactly where I lost it. I was in the lobby, and I took it off because it was rather warm, and hooked it over my purse. But I must've dropped it."

He continued to chew on his pinky fingernail. "Yeah?" He wasn't interested in the least.

"And the next thing I know, I saw a woman, in the aisle in front of me, wearing it. And I thought, *How funny. She has the same stole I have!"* Diana threw up her hands dramatically. "Which is impossible, because it was one of a kind! But I never realized it then. She must've seen me drop it and stolen it!"

He squinted. "She stole a stole?"

Diana nodded. "If only I'd had the sense to realize I'd dropped it and confronted her then!" She sniffled. "Now, it's too late. If only I could find the woman's name and address. Then I could visit her and ask her to return it."

He spit out a little bit of fingernail and shrugged. "Yeah."

Okay, kid. Time to get the hint.

But hc just continued to stare blankly at her. "Sorry that happened to you."

Great. Sheila, the other box office attendant, would be back soon, and then she'd probably never be able to get the information. She glanced at the computer. "Hey," she said as if it was a ncw idea that had just occurred to her. "Is the information of all the ticket purchasers on the computer?"

"Uh . . . yeah, sure."

"You wouldn't be able to look in there and tell me who had the seat, if I told you which one it was, would you?"

He hesitated, then looked out the door, where the girl had left. "I could do that, but I really don't think I'm supposed to."

"Oh. But my stole . . ." she sniffled a little.

He rolled his eyes, wheeled the chair over, and sat in it, scooting himself to the computer. "Fine. Let me just find it." He typed a few things in and pulled up a seating chart. "What seat did you think it was?"

She did the calculation in her head as she moved forward and sat on the edge of the desk. "Middle. Probably row two, H? Maybe I? I think it was a single ticket, like mine."

He moved the mouse around and scanned the results. "I've got a single ticket, but that was given, no cost, to a member of the orchestra."

"So . . . does that mean you don't have a name for the person who was sitting there?"

"I didn't say that. It's here. We take down the names of everyone who gets a ticket now, for security purposes. It's Nina Horvath, *Floridusgasse* 56."

"Oh! Thanks," she said, reaching for a piece of paper from a note dispenser and a pen from a cup. "Do you mind?"

"No," he said as she wrote it down, then quickly closed out of it.

"Thanks!" she said, tucking the paper into her pocket. "This is a huge help!"

"Sure. I hope you get it back."

She almost said, *Get what back?* but then she remembered the stole. "Oh! I hope so, too. Fingers crossed."

She reached the door just as the other box office clerk was returning. "Have a good day," she said innocently to the woman as she swept past her.

Diana had a date with Nina Horvath, even if the woman didn't know it.

CHAPTER THIRTEEN

It turned out that *Floridusgasse* 56 was within walking distance of the music hall. Following the directions on her GPS, Diana found herself across the street from *Burggarten*, the former Habsburg private garden that was now a conservatory and butterfly house. Supposedly, with its old trees, blooms and many monuments, it was one of the loveliest gardens, anywhere. It'd been on her original bucket list. She looked up from her phone and saw the Mozart monument out front, among a riot of color from the many blooming flowers.

I'll stop on the way back, she told herself.

Locating the street Nina Horvath lived on, she meandered down the tree-lined street, looking for number fifty-six. As she did, she stopped at the sight of a newspaper vending machine, on the corner. The front headline of the paper read, in glaring black block print: LUKAS HUBER MORD.

She didn't even have to guess what that meant. But wow, news moved quickly in this part of Austria. She understood the morning news carrying word of the murder, but the newspapers, too?

When she found the right house, she gazed up at it, a narrow but well-kept home with a gray stone façade. *I wonder what a young, single woman like her does in order to afford a place like this?* Diana wondered as she climbed the steps.

She rang the doorbell.

Not a moment later, the woman answered, wearing what looked like yoga gear. She was fit and trim, muscular, definitely—but was she the type of woman who would have had the strength for strangulation? She had her curls up in a messy bun at the top of her head, and no make-up at all. Her eyes were red-rimmed—had she been crying? Before, Diana had placed the woman at mid-twenties, but now, she looked like barely a teenager.

Nina squinted, then shook her head, a hint of disgust on her face. "*Das interessiert mich nicht.*"

Did she think Diana was selling something? She was about to close the door, but Diana spoke up. "No . . . I'm not. Here to sell you anything. I just came from *Musikverein.* I was at the Vienna Philharmonic performance last night. I believe I saw you last night? You were there, as well?"

Her brow wrinkled with worry. "I was. I went to Huber's performance. But I told everything to the police already."

"They contacted you?"

"Yes. They were here this morning." She frowned. "You are not with them, then? Who do you work for?"

"No one. I was actually at the performance last night, too. I was in the back right before Lukas Huber died. I saw you there."

"Yes . . . I was." She seemed even more confused. "But I had nothing to do with his death, if that's what you're insinuating. I barely even knew the man. I wasn't a fan of his music."

That felt like a lie, considering how they'd whispered to one another. "Oh? You seemed quite close, last night."

She snorted. "Perhaps we were."

"You've been crying, though."

She sighed. "Well, it was a shock! I was just with him. And we were . . . intimate."

"I thought you just said that . . ." Diana stopped as the pieces clicked together. "Are you telling me he . . ." Her eyes widened.

"Yes. He engaged my services." The woman shrugged, without a hint of shame. "Look. I don't know. I heard it was customary for Huber to hire a woman to keep him company prior to any performance. It loosened him up, they said. But that was my first time; he requested me."

"He requested you?"

"Yes. From the service I work for. Angels Vienna. That's the one he uses. It's not unusual to get calls from strange men, but I had heard Huber's name before. He's used a few of us. I suppose he just found my picture on the website."

Diana frowned. "I find that interesting that he'd hire an escort, considering he had so much obvious, um, interest from women, you know . . . afterwards. It's not like he needed to pay someone."

She smiled. "Most men who hire me don't like the entanglements, if you know what I mean."

Diana nodded. "So when was the last time you saw him?"

"Right after the performance. He asked me to stay around for a little bit, but once the rest of the crowd cleared out, he told me he wouldn't be needing me anymore. He paid me well, gave me a nice tip, and I left the concert hall on my own, just before ten." She shrugged. "That's what I told the police, too."

Diana stood there, trying to take it in. She sounded sincere. "Can anyone confirm that?"

"Sure can. Because since it was still early, I booked another appointment. With a gentleman in East Vienna. One of my regulars. I was at the Hotel Melia from about ten-fifteen until two-thirty. And if you don't believe me, you can ask to see their lobby tapes. I'm sure I'm on video there. At least, that's what I told the police."

So she wasn't getting any further than the police had. She frowned. "And that's it?"

"Yes. Around three, I got home and went to bed. Nothing more I can tell you. So of course this morning when my door's being beaten down, and when I heard the news from the police, I was afraid. I wondered who could do such a thing. He was a big head, thought he could do no wrong, was only a mediocre lover, but he did not deserve to die."

"Were you in his dressing room?"

She nodded. "Like I said. Before the performance. And yes, he was a jerk. Wanting things just so, if you know what I mean. But I've had worse clients, that is for certain."

"So then . . . did you see anyone acting strange?"

She laughed. "I saw *all* of them acting strange. All of those fans of his, crazy women. Taking off their panties and giving them to him, acting like they were at some kind of hard rock concert. They were awful! I've never seen such a thing in all my life. One of them even threatened me, because I was so close to him. I have no idea how he could not only live with that kind of obsessive attention, but enjoy it. It's terrible!"

"One of them threatened you?"

She nodded.

"Who?"

"A blonde woman. She had a braid down her back. Seemed like Lukas knew her, because he called her by name. Pia. That was it. He told me he'd met her at a lecture or benefit or something he did at the MDW—"

"MDW?"

“Oh, the University of Music and Performing Arts Vienna. She was a piano student there, and she wouldn’t stop following him around afterwards. She’d show up at his concerts, because she had special passes because she was a student. She didn’t miss one, and afterwards, she’d hang around, wanting to talk to him. Drove him mad, he said. She was in love, absolutely *obsessed* with Lukas Huber—or so he said.”

Diana blinked. This sounded promising. “Pia, you say? And you said she threatened you? How?”

Nina rolled her eyes. “Oh, she said I should keep my hands off Lukas if I knew what was good for me. I didn’t think it was serious, at the time. But now . . . who knows?”

“Was she in that back room, when Lukas was signing?”

She nodded. “Yeah. That was when she threatened me.” She tilted her head. “Wait . . . I know you from somewhere. Why are you asking these questions? Are you a friend of Huber’s?”

“No, I’m—”

“Ah, I know you now! You’re the one who told him off, right to his face! Ha, ha! I loved that,” she said, clapping her hands. “You told him that he was a pompous jerk whose head wouldn’t fit on the stage with the orchestra. That was a good one. And you’re totally right.”

She slapped her knee. Diana smiled. “Yes, well—”

“Did you take him up on his proposition?”

So she’d heard that? “No, of course not. I—"

“Wait. You were part of that group of crazy women who wanted their programs and bodies signed by him. Are you a big fan of his?”

Diana shook her head. “Not really. I just wanted to have my program signed as a keep—”

“Do you know something the police do not?” A sly smile spread across her pretty features. “You seem like a smart one. I bet you figure it out way before those dummies.”

After the conversation she’d had with Officer Moser earlier that day, where he shut down her theories, she tended to agree with Nina. “Thanks. That depends. Tell me, did you tell the officers about this woman, Pia?”

She tapped her chin. “Come to think of it, no. I didn’t. They didn’t ask me who I thought did it, or I would have. I don’t think she had a seat at the concert, either. She somehow sneaked in because she had special admission, for standing room only, as part of the University of

Music and Performing Arts Vienna. That's what I heard her tell someone."

"That's interesting," Diana said. *Because it means that the police won't be asking her questions. And only I can.* "As far as the University of Music and Performing Arts Vienna . . . where is it? Do you know?"

She smiled and spun her finger. "Just turn around and march right back where you came from. The conservatory is right across the street from *Musikverein.*"

"Oh. Thank you!"

"No problem. I hope you catch the killer before the police do," she said with a smile, closing the door. *"Schönen Tag!"*

Diana climbed the steps to the sidewalk and wandered toward the Mozart statue at *Burggarten,* which she promised she'd do. As she walked, she jabbed things into the Google search bar on her phone. *Pia Piano University of Music and Performing Arts Vienna.*

Quite a few search results came up, including one, with a pretty blonde girl, standing next to her piano, named Pia Zimmerman. She was a student in her third year at the University of Music and Performing Arts Vienna.

"That looks promising," she murmured as she studied the girl's face. "I bet—"

She stopped when she nearly collided face first with a lamp post. Sidestepping it, she continued on.

When she got to the base of the statue, she looked up at the marble image of Mozart. He stood there, blank-eyed, as statues often were, one hand turning over the sheet music on the stand next to him. A real pigeon perched atop his head, which made Diana think of Papageno from *The Magic Flute*. On the front relief, were two scenes she recognized from his opera, *Don Giovanni,* as well as an assemblage of instruments.

"So what do you think, Mr. Mozart?" she asked the statue. "Shall we go and speak to this Pia Zimmerman?"

Maybe it was because she was overtired, but she could've sworn she saw the statue's head nod slightly. She looked around. The last thing she needed was Detective Moser, seeing her talking with another dead musician.

All right, she thought, bowing her head solemnly to the great composer and turning on her heel. *Pia Zimmerman. Let's go back to Musikverein and see what she knows.*

CHAPTER FOURTEEN

By the time Diana made it back toward *Musikverein*, it was almost noon. Despite the large Viennese breakfast she'd had, her stomach was rumbling. There was a food truck across the street, at the park, so she got a Bratwurst and nibbled it while watching a string quartet, playing an impromptu concert. She listened as they played Josef Haydn's String Quartet in C Major, Op. 76, No. 3, the Emperor Hymn, smiling as a small crowd gathered, listening to the mournful song.

Her heart soared. That was the way music was, to her. Weekends at her grandparents' home would always fly by because she'd constantly be listening to the music. By the time the performance was over, her Bratwurst was gone without her even remembering finishing it, and she'd almost forgotten the reason she'd come back to this spot.

As the crowd applauded, Diana noticed that the cellist was wearing a t-shirt with a logo emblazoned on it for the University of Music and Performing Arts Vienna. *Of course. Maybe he knows Pia Zimmerman.*

She approached him. "That was wonderful! You're beautiful performers. I'm very moved."

He looked up from the case, where he was settling his instrument and bow. He seemed embarrassed. "Thank you. I am glad you liked it." He motioned to *Musikverein.* "We played it in honor of the Great Lukas Huber. A terrible loss to our community. Whenever one of our own falls, we always play a concert of remembrance here."

"Oh. Yes. I know," she said. "Very sad. You sounded lovely together, the four of you. You attend the conservatory?"

He nodded. "First year."

"Have you seen Huber perform?"

He nodded. "He was always playing concerts for us students. He attended the university for a time, so he was always around here, kind of like a fixture. I didn't know him well; I've only been here a year. But a lot of people at the school feel the loss greatly."

"I understand. You wouldn't happen to know Pia Zimmerman? She'd be a third year student, I believe, in piano?"

He snapped the cello's case closed and lifted it up. "I know her, yes."

"Would you happen to know where she is? I met her last night, at the performance, and—"

"You were there?" His eyes bulged. "I didn't know she was, but I guess it makes sense. From what I hear, he was one of her main influences."

"Yes, and well, I wanted to ask her—"

"She's probably just getting out of performance right now. She tutors first-years. In the main building. Theater." He pointed across the street from the *Musikverein*, at a nondescript marble structure. There were a few banners outside, with the same crest that was on his t-shirt.

"Great! *Danke!"* she said, hurrying off, across the street.

She walked into the grand building. Several young students were there, carrying their instruments, chatting, or reading in the various nooks and benches around the main lobby. The theater wasn't hard to find; there were sets of double doors, directly across from the entrance. No one bothered to ask her for identification, and she made it to the theater doors without being noticed by a single soul.

The second she opened the door, she heard it. Riotous piano music, lively and light, exploded from the front of the theater.

This theater was nothing like the one she'd been in last night. It was modern, sparse, and more utilitarian than decorative. Diana made her way down the aisle until she saw the blonde, so captivated by her performance, her body moving with each note, that she might not have noticed an earthquake shaking underneath her. It was a melody Diana had never heard before, but the piece seemed ridiculously fast and difficult. And yet the woman-- Pia Zimmerman—seemed to pull it off with all the grace that Lukas Huber had, but with none of the swagger.

When she finished, she sat there, still, for a moment, staring almost despondently at the piano keys, as if she wasn't entirely satisfied with her performance.

Diana said, her voice echoing through the theater. "That was amazing." When the girl didn't look up, she added, "I wasn't familiar with the piece, though?"

"La Campanella," she said quietly, staring at the keys. "Liszt. It'd be better if I had bigger hands."

"I didn't notice. I mean, I'm no musician, but it sounded great."

When she turned to look at Diana, it was obvious that she'd been crying, too. Her eyes were clearly bloodshot. *Wow. The big ego broke hearts all over this town.*

Her voice was cold. "This is a closed practice."

"Yes. I'm sorry, but I--

"What do you want?" She pulled her legs out from under the piano and stood up. "If you need the stage, I'm on my way—"

"No. I came to talk to you. Pia, right?"

She stopped. "Yes. About what?"

"Last night. You were at the performance, weren't you?"

She froze. Swallowed. "Yes. Yes I was. I've been to every one of Lukas Huber's performances in Vienna in the last two years." She sniffed. "I was his biggest fan."

"I'm sorry. You must be devastated."

"I am. He was a genius. One of the greatest musicians known to man." She looked at the piano. "I wanted to be like him. Did you ever hear *him* play La Campanella? *He* has the hands."

That sounded a bit like jealousy. But was she jealous enough to commit murder over it? Maybe she'd snapped and killed him, even though he was her idol. "I heard his compositions have been compared to Liszt."

She shrugged. "I don't really see the comparison in their compositions. Huber's work is far more polished, with a quality, a sensuality that can't be explained. But Huber was more like Liszt as a person."

"What does that mean?"

Her lips twisted. "When Liszt burst out onto the scene in Berlin in the mid 1800s, he was a virtual rock star. After his concerts, women began fighting over his cigarette butts, handkerchiefs and gloves. They'd wear his portrait on brooches and cameos, close to their heart."

"Ah. I see. Huber definitely had his female fans, from what I've heard."

She scowled. "Unfortunately."

"How did you think he did last night?"

"Oh, so good. He was at his best. And his Jupiter Symphony?" Her lips trembled. "I'm sure it'll be remembered forever. It's a masterpiece."

Well, I'm not sure I'd go that far. "I had a seat in the hall. I didn't see you there."

She nodded. "That's because students of the university get free admission. Standing room. In the back. There's a place for any of us who want to attend. That was one of the things Lukas made sure of."

"But you were admitted into the back to congratulate him, last night? After the performance?"

She shrugged. "Security is notoriously lax during performances, but from what I hear, that's Lukas Huber's way. He never believed in having tight security, because he wants to be accessible to fans. I've always been able to get into the back if I leave right during the final bows. They never see me. So yes, I was there. I spoke to him."

"You did?"

"I told him he was great. And he told me he was hoping I'd come. He was so sweet." She let out a little sob. "He was really . . . an amazing artist. So selfless with his time. Always at the university, helping out."

"He was?" Diana asked, genuinely surprised. The man she'd met last night didn't seem like the type to be very generous with his time, unless a pretty woman was involved. *Maybe I misjudged him?*

She nodded. "That's why it's such a . . ."

She brought her hand to her face and started to weep into it.

Diana reached into her purse and pulled out a tissue. She went to the stage and held it up to the girl, who bent slightly to take it. "Thank you. Sorry. He just means a lot to me. To all of us at the university. I feel a little lost, now. He used to be a fixture on the campus. I can't believe that I won't go to the Opus café on the corner and see him there, in his window booth."

That didn't sound like the voice of a murderer. It sounded like someone who was deeply affected by the man's loss. "When did you last see him?"

"Well, I . . ." Pia stopped and frowned. "Why are you asking? Who are you?"

"I'm someone who cares and wants to see justice done. Like you. I want to know what happened," Diana said gently. "I think he deserves that much. So that his family and loved ones and all the people who cared about him, throughout the world, can have their peace."

Okay, Diana, stop laying it on so thick.

But it worked, because Pia nodded. "Yes. I hope the killer is found. Where was I?" She looked up, thinking. "I guess I left pretty early.

Like nine-thirty. I didn't stay more than a few minutes. I saw him, spoke to him, and then I went home. I had an exam to study for."

"Did you talk to anyone else?" Diana said, thinking of what Nina had told her about the threat she'd made.

She bit her lip, tossed her braid in front of her shoulder. "No . . . I don't think so . . ."

"I spoke to a woman who said she thought she talked to you. A Nina Horvath? That's why I'm here. She was dark-haired, pretty, a companion of Lukas's, probably . . ."

Her eyes narrowed. "Oh, right. The distraction of the week." She rolled her eyes. "Yes, I spoke to her."

"She said you threatened her."

Pia's eyes went wide. "No, I didn't. At least, I didn't *mean* to. She thought she was something special, hanging onto him like she owned him. She's wrong."

"Is she?"

"Likely. Every performance, Lukas always has a certain number of seats in the front, set aside. For his many women. But he's never been serious about any of them. Usually. He collects them. Makes love to them. It isn't unusual to see them fighting over him, backstage. He loves it. That's why he doesn't like security getting in the way. I think it's his entertainment."

Diana watched her talking, as if she was his best friend. *She's also talking about him like he's still alive. Like she doesn't believe he's really gone.*

"The thing is, everyone knows, the floozies are a threat to his music. His creation. He's fond of telling people that he needs a woman to be his muse. Bach, Wagner, Stravinsky were all the same—the passion for music becomes passion for other things, and the two feed each other. But I promise you, for Lukas, it's not the same. Five years ago, supposedly, he fell in love with one of the girls, and he didn't create *the entire time."*

This was news. She didn't realize that man could love anyone but himself. But if he was volunteering his time and falling in love with women, maybe there was a gentler side to him she hadn't noticed. Diana stared at the young piano student, waiting for more context. When it didn't come, she said, "And that's bad?"

"Worse than bad! Here's a guy who was used to churning out a symphony in his sleep, at least once a week. He was seriously prolific.

And then a floozy came along and ruined it for him," she said with a shake of the head. "So the last thing that he needs is to fall in love with anyone else. Also, I kind of was hoping he'd take me under his wing, and I could study under him, learn his secrets, and I knew that wasn't going to happen as long as he was chasing tail all around Vienna. So that's why I told her she should get lost. But I didn't mean him or the floozy any harm. I promise, I didn't." Her eyes narrowed. "Wait. Did she say I did?"

"No, she didn't," Diana lied, not wanting to escalate. "She just mentioned that she saw you there. Do you have any idea who could've done this?"

She shrugged. "Other than Floozy A, B, C or D, no. Take your pick from them. They're all winners."

"Do you remember any of the other floozies—uh, I mean women?"

She shook her head. "Nope. He had a definite type, though. Gorgeous. Thin. Big boobs."

That didn't narrow things down much. Perfect. Pia and Nina were essentially both naming each other as the chief suspect. So that left Diana with a big sack of . . . nothing. No leads.

"Well, thank you for your time," Diana said, nodding at her. "I'll let you get back to your practicing."

"Thank you," said Pia, and as Diana headed toward the back of the theater, she began to play the Rondo Alla Turca, the Turkish March from Mozart's Piano Sonata No. 11. Another one of Diana's most favorite pieces, she'd have loved to see the woman play.

But there were other things on her mind now, besides the music. Her mind twisted with theories and possibilities as she made her way out into the summer sun.

Diana wandered off the university grounds, nonplussed. Her investigation had come to a thudding halt. *I suppose I could do some sightseeing now,* she said, pulling out her phone. *What should I see?*

She'd just decided to stroll the gardens of Belvedere Palace when she looked up and saw a small café on the corner . . . Café Opus.

Something tickled in the back of her mind. She'd heard of that before, quite recently. But from who?

As she stared in the window, the answer came to her. *Are you really suffering from short-term memory loss, Diana? You heard it a few minutes ago. Pia said Lukas Huber used to frequent the place.*

Seizing the last threads of hope of ever finding out anything about this murder, she went inside.

CHAPTER FIFTEEN

The café was very small, and most of the people were probably no more than half Diana's age. Even though she didn't fit in, no one looked at her. They were all busy reading their music, sipping their drinks, and chatting, their music cases by their sides.

She found a free table near the counter and the pretty, waifish barista, probably a student herself with a short black pixie cut and a nose ring, looked at her. *"Wie kann ich Ihnen helfen?"*

Diana assumed that was some version of, *Can I help you?* Her stomach was still full from the Bratwurst, so she only ordered a mélange.

As the barista went to fill her order, Diana looked around. She noticed several copies of the newspaper, announcing his death, sprawled out on the modern tables and chairs, and someone had constructed a memorial to him, which was simply his picture, propped up near the sugar, creamer, and stirrers. His dark eyes gazed at Diana in a discomforting way. *Help me, Diana. Solve the mystery of my death.*

She looked away as the barista pushed a frothing mug over to her. The woman probably knew just as much as the next person about Lukas Huber, but Diana decided it was the only shot she had. She pointed to the photograph. "So. Sad news, huh?"

The girl shrugged. "Not really."

Diana raised an eyebrow. "You're not a music fan?"

She laughed. "No. I am. I attend the university. But he was not a nice man. He'd stay in his booth over there—" she motioned with her chin to a place in the corner "—for hours, demanding refills again and again, and then he'd leave pennies for a tip. I don't like to speak ill of the dead, but he was not nice. No one here really liked him."

Diana pointed at the picture. "But—"

"Okay, *some* people liked him," she corrected. "He was obviously a talented man. The pride of the Vienna Philharmonic. So if they liked him, they liked him for that. Not for the person he was. He treated everyone as if he was better than them. And do you know how many times he squeezed my butt while I was pouring him coffee? I probably have permanent scars!"

Diana nodded and leaned in to sample her drink. It was steaming, so she braced herself for a burnt lip. The girl's impression sounded very similar to her own perception of him—he was a complete ego.

Then the barista added, "But he wasn't the most talented the Vienna Philharmonic had. That's for sure. They could do better. They *have* done better."

Diana winced as her lip hit the too-hot liquid, and pulled back, in simultaneous pain and surprise. "What do you mean?"

"Well, he grew up here, but he went away for most of his training, and when he came back, a few years ago, he took Vienna by storm. Everyone just adored him, so the Philharmonic used him more and more, casting their long-standing lead pianist to the side. He sold tickets, not that *Musikverein* needed help with that, but an in-demand act always gets more publicity. And he was clearly their golden goose. But most people forget that they had to sideline a very talented pianist in order to take him on."

"Who was that?"

"My Uncle. Gunther Graf. You've heard of him?"

She shook her head. "Should I have?"

The girl snorted. "I guess not. He was only the Philharmonic's principal pianist for three decades. He was incredible. And yet this hotshot Huber bursts out onto the stage, with all his flash and irreverence, and steals the seat out from under him. The excuse they gave him was that they needed fresh blood."

Diana leaned forward, now keenly interested. *I smell a motive.* "When did this happen?"

"Oh, just about six months ago," she said. "My poor uncle was absolutely devastated. He worked so hard to get where he was, and he felt like he was appreciated. Then, BANG. It was over."

"That's terrible."

The girl's face was now red with indignation. "Yeah. And the thing is, Lukas Huber wasn't a very good pianist, really. He was sloppy. His technique was off. He didn't put the right emotion in the pieces. He played every piece angry, coldly. My uncle interpreted the music far differently, and in my opinion, in a better way, with so much more emotion. Listen to their recordings side-by-side, if you get a chance. You'll see what I mean."

Diana already knew what she meant. Lukas Huber was handsome and charming and a joy to look at, but there was something missing in her music, a *je ne sais quoi* that hadn't been able to deliver the perfectly immersive experience that would've pulled the tears from her eyes. "Your uncle was devasted, you say?"

She nodded, but then her eyes widened. "Yes, but if you're thinking he was jealous and wanted to get some kind of revenge on Lukas Huber for taking his place in the orchestra, don't bother. My uncle is the most gentle man on Earth. He wouldn't hurt a fly."

"No?"

"No. He retired to a little place in the south of the city and is very happy with his quiet life and his vegetable garden. Trust me. Do you want another one?"

Diana looked down. Somehow, without knowing, she'd sucked down the rest of her drink. No wonder her tongue felt scalded, and the roof of her mouth was raw. "No. Thank you."

The woman wrote the check and handed it to her as Diana thought. Growing up, she'd once had an uncle who was the fun-loving, life of the party at holiday get-togethers. He'd put lottery tickets under their plates at Christmas and make everyone play crazy card games for silly prizes. Every get-together was more fun with Uncle Lou. As a child, she'd loved him—he'd been her favorite uncle, by far.

And then Uncle Lou was arrested for embezzling nearly a million dollars from the company he worked for. Apparently, he'd played other games, ones that weren't necessary legal.

The point was, sometimes, people thought the best of their family members. But the side a person showed one's family wasn't necessarily who they were to the rest of the world. Gunther Graf might have had a mean, jealous streak his niece knew nothing about.

She grabbed her purse and pulled out a few euros. As she set them down, she thought, *Gunther Graf. I need to remember that name. That's my next lead.*

The barista took her money and turned to the cash register. As she did, Diana thought of another question. "Oh. Do you think it's possible one of his female admirers might have killed him?"

She shrugged. "It's possible. I heard he had a lot of those. He always had some of the female college girls flapping and preening around him as he sat in his booth. He liked it; encouraged it. I don't get what people saw in him. He was a small man with a big ego."

"Oh. Okay." She shuffled her backside to the edge of the stool. "Th—"

Her phone buzzed. She stopped, fished it out of her pocket, and stared at the screen. She hadn't looked at it since she came in, but there were already five messages and phone calls, littering the display. All of them were from Lily. How had she not heard her ringing her, before? She'd had her phone on silent, but usually, she could feel the buzz.

She opened the series of messages and her eyes caught on the last message. Her stomach dropped: *MOM. WHERE ARE YOU? IT'S AN EMERGENCY. CALL ME NOW.*

CHAPTER SIXTEEN

Diana rushed out into the street and quickly dialed her eldest daughter's number, fearing the worst. Lily was pregnant. Only about twenty weeks along. Was something wrong with the baby? As much as Diana dreaded the idea of being referred to as "Grandma" she couldn't deny that she was thrilled about the coming addition, so thrilled, she vowed to fly back to the States, to welcome the little one to the world, the moment her eldest went into labor.

So at that moment, as the phone rang, Diana's entire life as Grandma flashed before her eyes. The moment she found out and squealed with glee. The time she'd gone to the doctor with Lily and met the peanut on the ultrasound. The time she'd bought the baby a little frock in Verona. A week ago, Lily had just been beginning to show.

She couldn't deny, though she had many destinations in Europe and things to do for herself on her bucket list, the baby was the thing she'd been looking forward to the *most*.

Annoyingly, the phone rang and rang, amping up Diana's nervousness. What if Lily had gone into the doctor and was now being operated on? Frantic, Diana was just about to hang up and call Mick, Lily's husband, when a completely unconcerned voice said, "Hello? Mom?"

"Lily!" she shouted, half-hysterical by then, half-relieved that Lily was still capable of speaking to her on the phone. "Are you okay? Did anything happen?"

"*No*, I am not okay," she muttered. "Not in the least."

Oh, no, Diana thought, despite the fact that Lily sounded okay, maybe there was something seriously wrong. "Is it the baby?"

She sniffled. "Yeah."

Diana looked up at the sky and said a quick prayer. "All right. It's okay. Whatever it is, you'll get through it. What is it? Did you go to the doctor?"

"Yeah. That's where we are now. I'm having an ultrasound."

Diana's heart skipped in her chest. They must have found an abnormality. Maybe it wasn't so bad. There had been abnormalities with Diana's ultrasound of Lily, too. She'd had gestational diabetes, and everyone told her that she'd have a huge baby, and she needed to be very careful to monitor the size of the baby so it didn't get too big. Lily had been born at just under six pounds. So maybe they didn't know everything.

She took a deep breath, trying to find the words to make her eldest feel better. "All right. Calm down. Exactly what did the doctor say?"

"Oh, they haven't said anything yet. I'm in the waiting room, waiting to be called in."

"Oh!" Diana hesitated, now thoroughly confused. "Um, so— what is wrong with the baby? Why are you having an ultrasound?"

"It's just my regular, planned ultrasound," she explained. "You know, twenty weeks? The problem is that I can't get Mick to agree with me. The big, stubborn mule. It's my body, right? So I should decide what we're doing."

"Back up. What are you talking about? Is the baby okay?"

"As far as I know, the baby inside my stomach is okay," she said sourly. "But right now, the baby sitting right next to me is about to get his face smacked."

Diana clutched at her heart. It was still beating madly in her chest. "What?"

"Can you believe he doesn't want to know the baby's sex? I told him I have to know! How else will we know how to decorate the nursery? I was thinking a Harry Potter theme. What do you think? But only if it's a boy. Otherwise--"

Diana frowned. There had to be more to it than that. Lily couldn't possibly be calling just because she and Mick were having a little argument that they needed her to settle for them. Did they really think this was an emergency? "Lily, you said it was an emergency. I thought something bad had happened."

"Mom. This *is* bad. Catastrophic, in fact. I'm about to go into the ultrasound room and I want to murder the father of this child. That is not boding well for our future, don't you think?"

"Lily. Have some perspective!" she practically shouted, only realizing she was talking loud when a couple of people on the street turned to look at her. Bea was her drama queen, but Lily also had her moments, especially when anything involving her health was involved.

"You are all healthy. Hope that the baby is healthy. As long as it is, really, Mick's right. The sex doesn't matter."

"I know, but—"

"But nothing. Lily. If you want to find out the sex, you can. But tell the technician to keep it from Mick. That's all. Easy. Okay?"

"Yeah, I guess. But don't you want to know? And what kind of man doesn't want to know the sex of his own child? It's like, doesn't he even care about this baby?"

Diana rolled her eyes. She knew Mick to be the guy who cared so much, he'd proven it in all sorts of ways during their decade-long relationship. The two had been childhood sweethearts. But Mick had never had a child before, so he was learning as he went. It seemed only normal that they'd get into fights from time to time. Diana had quite a few similar disagreements with Evan. "Dear, he's the kind of man who doesn't care what sex it is, as long as it's healthy. That's a good thing. And of course, I want to know. But I'll wait until you're ready to tell me, all right?"

"Yes, but sometimes I just feel like—"

"I'd love to hear how things go. Remember, it's normal to feel a little vulnerable, to have all those strong emotions during your pregnancy. We talked about this, right?" Before her daughter could answer, she added, "But I have a little too much on my plate right now to worry about settling an argument between you two. Just compromise. I know you two can do it."

"Mom! You're still in Vienna, aren't you? What, am I disrupting your all-important sightseeing schedule?"

"I haven't seen many sights at all, to be honest," she admitted. "You see, there's a murder investigation going on, with the police breathing down my neck, and—"

"What, again?" Lily sounded as though Diana had just missed a connecting flight somewhere—strangely nonchalant, as if this was only a minor annoyance, as opposed to something that could land her in jail for a long time. "You're joking. You have to be joking."

"Unfortunately, I'm not joking."

"That sounds like a repeat of what you went through in Verona. What happened?"

"Well, I went to *Musikverein* last night, and the pianist was particularly good. I went into the back to tell him that I enjoyed his performance and found him dead. He'd been murdered. So naturally, they think I did it, since I found the body. It doesn't help that I've been involved in other murders in Europe. They're a bit suspicious."

"I bet. You've been finding more dead people than living people, I think. I told you to stay away from ax murderers when you went out there. I had no idea you'd be accused of being one, yourself."

"He was not chopped to bits with an ax, Dear." There Lily went with her abundant ax murdering theories, again. "He was strangled."

"Strangled? Well, same thing. That's really brutal! Like you could do a thing like that. I can't believe these people constantly think you're responsible. What evidence do they have?"

Diana leaned against the café's exterior in the shade of a tree. "Not very much, but I have a bit of a motive."

"A motive? For killing a strange pianist? What possible motive could you—"

"I had an altercation with him prior to his death. And since I found h—"

"Mom! I knew you'd flipped your lid when you decided to go off on this vacation, but now you're provoking Austrian men? What's gotten into you?

"Nothing! I—"

"I knew this trip would be trouble. What kind of altercation?"

"Oh, he was treating some of his young fans abominably, and had a bit of an ego. I couldn't stand for it! What he did to this one little boy who was his fan . . . it was terrible. I just wanted to put him in his place. Not murder him. But of course, everyone saw the exchange, so I became suspect number one."

"They don't have anyone else?"

"Not that I know of. I'm trying to steer clear of the police . . ."

"You should. But what they have on you sounds really flimsy. Like you would even be able to do—" She cut off, and for a moment, Diana thought she might've lost the connection, until she said, "Stop it Mick. Come on. It's not a big deal. It's fine."

"Is everything—"

"Yes. Mick just read something in a brochure about the dangers of eating cold cuts. He was upset because I ate a deadly turkey club yesterday at lunch. He thinks I'm going to get listeriosis. I don't even know what that is!"

"Oh, well it can be bad for the baby. You should probably stay away from—"

She stopped when she realized Lily wasn't listening. She was conversing with Mick, their voices muffled.

"He tells me it can be bad for the baby. So, fine. No more turkey clubs. I already have so many things that I can't or won't eat, because they gross me out. Now I'll just have to add turkey clubs to the list." She sighed. "So what else do the cops have, besides you fighting with the victim?"

Diana blinked at how quickly Lily could flit between subjects. She was always the business-minded one, good at balancing a lot of plates. "Let's see. Not very much, except that I found him, in his dressing room."

"You did? Gruesome! Wait . . . didn't you find that other guy, dead in his dressing room, in Verona? What are the chances?"

Diana didn't want to be reminded of that. Yes, it was an odd coincidence, and probably gave the police every reason to suspect her. She could just imagine the headlines: *American Tourist Serial Killer Murdering European Performers Backstage!* "Yes, I'll admit it is strange. But that time, I was in the dressing room when the actor dropped dead. This time, I just found the man dead. I left for a while after the fight, and then I returned, but just to get my program signed. I found him lying on the floor, strangled with his cravat. They think that's—"

"Hold on." Lily disappeared again. Then she came back. "I've got to go. They want me in for the appointment. Hold on, Mick!"

Diana sighed. If it had been her youngest daughter, nothing would've torn her from the phone. Bea would've made time, because solving mysteries and batting about theories was her favorite activity. Bea had been her sidekick last week, and instrumental in finding the killer in Verona. She'd been like the Watson to her Sherlock, because of her love of Agatha Christie novels. Bea was an out-of-the-box thinker, so her theories had helped.

Lily's mind didn't work that way. She had a mind for business, which was why she ran a successful business as a realtor on Long Island. She was practical, careful.

Well, except when she'd nearly given Diana a heart attack with those text messages. That had been anything but careful. In fact, Diana was lucky she hadn't passed out right on this Austrian street corner.

"All right. Good luck. Text me photos of the peanut! And give Mick my best."

"I will. Bye Mom. And don't do anything crazy. Just go along with whatever the police say and be careful! I don't want you getting in any trouble! Especially with a murderer on the loose!"

"Of course. Believe me, I know how to handle the police by now," she said, ending the call and letting out a sigh of relief. *As for the murderer, well, I don't even know who that is, right now.*

I'm so glad the baby's okay. Now that that all-important emergency fizzled, it's time to deal with a REAL emergency.

Diana quickly thumbed in the name of the pianist, Gunther Graf. All she had to do was find out his address.

No information came up. But that was okay. Her good friend Dieter at the *Musikverein* box office would probably be able to help with that. After all, Gunther Graf had worked with the Vienna Philharmonic for thirty years. They had to have his address on file.

She smiled. *I'm sure he won't mind if I just stop by and ask a few questions.*

But just as she took a single step in that direction, she looked up across the street and saw a familiar face, atop a muscular body that was thundering toward her. A familiar, *terrifying* face.

It was Officer Moser, and he did not look the least bit happy.

CHAPTER SEVENTEEN

Diana shifted from foot to foot as the man approached, his face as stony and frightening as the Terminator himself. Next to him was a slightly shorter and leaner, dark-skinned man in a neat black suit and dark sunglasses. *Talk about intimidating,* Diana thought as the two men surrounded her, arms crossed over their broad chests. They were more than a head taller than her, blocking out the sun's rays. Anyone on the street who witnessed it probably thought she'd done something *really* bad, that they had to use such manpower on little ol' her.

"Mr. Moser," she squeaked out, nodding at the detective first, and then the other man. "Hello. To what do I owe the pleasure?"

Moser motioned to the man beside him. "This is Marius Ugbodu, from Interpol."

Diana stared. "Interpol?"

The man spoke in an impossibly deep voice, with a bit of a British accent. "Yes, Detective Moser was concerned about a murder you may have witnessed?"

She couldn't help blurting out the first thing that came to mind. "Which one?"

She cringed. That probably wasn't the best thing to say.

The two men exchanged looks. Ugbodu pulled a notepad from his breast pocket and said, "Let's start with the first one. Where was that?"

"Paris. About a month and a half ago. At the Versailles costumed ball. A man was pushed from a balcony and—"

"I know of that one. It involved the robbery of the *Madam Royale* diamond, is that right?" Ugbodu said, looking up from his notepad.

"Right. The murderer was found, as was the robber. I had nothing to do with it. I mean, I was wearing the jewel for a time, and then I danced with the thief, but in the end, it was just a case of being in the wrong place at the wrong time," she explained.

"As were you during the second murder?" Detective Moser asked.

She shrugged. "That one was in Verona. An actor. A member of his troupe killed him. Typical jealous actor. I had the misfortune of being in his dressing room when it happened. Poisoning."

Ugbodu wrote this down. “And again, during this third murder, you were seen nearby?” He scratched his pronounced, square jawline. “This is a remarkable coincidence.”

“Not too remarkable, if you know me,” she said, her teeth chattering nervously as she tried to smile. “I don’t know what it is. I’ve been the queen of bad luck, on this trip, it seems.”

They didn’t return her smile. Not that she expected them to, by this time. She stiffened.

“Why are you here?” Ugbodu asked, his tone accusatory.

“Here? You mean, here on this street, or here in this country?”

He must’ve though she was being facetious, because his scowl deepened. “Both.”

“Just vacation. I’ve been taking a year-long holiday through Europe.”

“And none of this bad luck has convinced you to go home,” he mused, writing something down on his pad.

“Well, I guess you can say I’m a tough nut to crack.” She smiled again.

Again, they did not return it.

She sighed. “Look. I know it looks bad. But I promise I had nothing to do with any of this. I suppose you summoned Interpol to arrest me as some international threat, but I promise you, I—”

“No,” Ugbodu said. “As an employee of Interpol, I work in accordance with the local law enforcement. I investigate possible connections and provide information. I don’t arrest anyone, Ma’am. That’s up to the local districts. But when we heard about you, we thought we should look into it.”

“Oh.” Somehow, that didn’t make her feel any better. “And what sort of information are you providing on me?”

He inhaled sharply. “I’m not at liberty to say.”

So that means that I have a file as a possible international terrorist, simply because I was in the wrong place at the wrong time. Thrice.

She looked at the detective. “Did you find anything else out about who could have killed Lukas Huber?”

He shook his head, his lips pinched. “No. But I did find that a certain American lady has been poking her nose where it doesn’t belong, interviewing people about the murder?” He shot her an accusing look. “I heard someone fitting your description was seen at the box office, earlier today.”

She couldn't deny it. "I was not poking. Well. Not really. I'm just curious. Besides, you clearly think I did it. And you wouldn't listen to any of my tips. You basically shut me down."

Ugbodu looked at him curiously, as if to say, *Is that true?* Moser grunted. "Your tip was to investigate someone we already had on my list. We have a lot of leads, Ma'am. And that one was obvious. Do you have anything *not* obvious?"

She thought about telling them about Gunther Graf, but stopped. She didn't really want to be told how obvious that one was. He'd been at the Vienna Philharmonic thirty years, only to be replaced by that wetback. He had a perfect motive.

"I guess not. And yet for all your leads, you seem to be spending a lot of time, questioning *me*. So pardon me, but if I can do something to find some clues to take the heat off me, I'm going to."

He raised an eyebrow, clearly taken aback by her monologue. She smiled proudly. *How's that for standing up for yourself? Good job, tiger!*

But then, Moser leaned in close to her ear and bit out the words, "*Frau* St. James?"

"Yes?"

"*Don't.*"

That was it. It was so terse, so short, an *I'll be back,* or *Hasta la vista, baby,* moment if she'd ever heard one. She felt her confidence crumple a little bit inside, like a used tissue.

He turned and started to walk away coolly, motioning to Ugbodu to follow him across the street.

Ugbodu nodded, reached into a fancy silver case and pulled out a business card. "Contact me if you think of anything that can help," he said, handing it to her.

Right. I know how that works. You only half-listen to me and then tell me to mind my own business, or only contact you when I think of something "not obvious." "Thank you," she said, tucking the card in her purse. "Are you helping the Detective look for who murdered Lukas Huber?"

He nodded. "Considering it is a very high-profile case, and he has several influential friends, his superiors want it solved as soon as possible."

"Well . . . good luck," she said. *I'll help . . . if I can. If you'll let me.*

He looked over his shoulder and then leaned in. "To you, also. But if I were you, I'd listen to Moser and stay away from any possible suspects. The police mean business. I'd say it's very suspicious of you, hanging around the location of the murder, interviewing people who knew Huber." It was as if he had read her mind. He tapped his silver case and placed it back in his breast pocket. "And from what I see about your history, they have good reason. You understand?"

She nodded. He turned around and headed across the street, following Moser.

Shaken, she stood there, frozen, words from the conversation repeating in her head. *If I were you . . . I'd stay away.* That sounded like more than just friendly advice.

It sounded like a threat.

With a bit of indignation, Diana crossed the street in the other direction and headed toward *Musikverein,* away from the officers. As she did, she gnawed on the inside of her cheek.

How dare they tell me where I can and can't go? Musikverein is the society of the friends of music. I am a friend of music! That's all! I'm not some murderer, returning to the scene of the crime, for goodness' sake!

She turned around, expecting to see them watching her. But they were gone. She let out a sigh of relief.

Dark clouds filled the sky as she went around the side of the massive building, thinking about what the woman had told her in Café Opus. Gunther Graf definitely had a motive to want Lukas Huber dead for taking his prized position as soloist in the Vienna Philharmonic. But had he?

She had to find out.

CHAPTER EIGHTEEN

Yes, Moser had told her to stay away. But she couldn't. Not when she had such a good lead on her hands. If she could just find out where Graf lived, she could go over there and ask him a few questions. Hopefully, Detective Moser had so many suspects on his list of leads that he hadn't gotten around to Graf, and she wouldn't run into him again.

She climbed the steps to *Musikverein* and went to the box office. There, she saw the same, acne-faced kid, sitting behind the glass, looking bored. "Hi, there!"

He stiffened when he saw her. "Uh," he said, his voice cracking like a preteen's, "I'm not supposed to let you in."

She looked around. He'd been so friendly before. "Who told you that?"

"Uh. . . my boss. Sheila. The police came by and said to be aware of some American lady, poking around, prying for information. That's you, right?"

Diana blinked. It was a wonder they hadn't plastered WANTED posters with her name on it, all over town. "Well, I don't—"

"Sheila said you probably didn't lose your stole at all! That you were looking for something else. Is that true?" He looked hurt at having been lied to.

She sighed. "Okay, I'll be honest with you. Yes, it's true. I was looking for the name of someone I thought I'd seen with Huber before he died. I'm sorry . . . what is your name, again?"

"Dieter."

She smiled at him sadly. "I'm sorry, Dieter. But to tell you the truth, I'm afraid. They seem to think I did it. When I didn't. And I only want to clear my name. But instead of looking at anyone else, they seem to be narrowing in on me. And I'm a little—actually, a lot—nervous. So I am very sorry that I lied to you. But could you understand?"

He sniffled and wiped his nose with the back of his hand. "Why do they think *you* did it, of all people? There were a thousand people in *Musikverein* last night. Why you?"

"Because I went into the back to get my program signed by him. And we had a bit of a confrontation."

"Confrontation?" A smile spread over his face. "Like what kind?"

"Oh, I just told him he'd never be Beethoven, or something like that," she said, much to his amusement.

"Ha!" He seemed to approve. "It's true. Good for you. And *that's* all they have on you? That won't hold up in court."

"Well, I did happen to find the body, and—"

"You did? Wild!" he said, excited. "What was it like? Was he all bloody and gross and bloated?"

She shook her head. "No. Actually, I didn't look very long. It was something I don't want to ever see—"

"Wait 'til I tell Sheila this! She'll go crazy when she hears this," Dieter said, pumping his fist excitedly. "Someone who actually saw the body. That's cool."

"Yeah . . . maybe you shouldn't tell her that I came back?"

He stared at her, uncomprehending.

"She's your boss, right? Well, after what the police said, if she knew I came back and you were talking to me, she might be . . ."

His eyes widened with understanding. "Ohhhh. Got you. Right." He winked as if the two of them were in some vast conspiracy together. "But I don't see how they could think *you* did it. Strangling someone? You're far too nice."

She smiled. "Well, thank y—"

"You're like my kindly old grandmother," he added.

Her face fell. Part of her wanted to explain that it would've had to be a miracle of science for him to be her grandchild, since her own children were just a few years older than him. But she didn't want to waste her time. It didn't matter. "Well, then, do you mind if I ask you a question?"

He shrugged.

"Gunther Graf. You know him?"

He nodded. "Well, not very well. I've been working here a long time, but he was kind of an old, quiet guy who didn't say much to anyone. Kept to himself. Nice, but all we ever said to each other was *Guten Tag*."

“So you were working here when he was fired?”

He nodded.

“And was there a disagreement over his being let go, did you know?”

“Disagreement? That’s putting it mildly. It was like a big blow-up. Everyone saw it. The only time I saw the billiard ball was when he was bouncing out the door. He slammed it so hard that all the panes in it shattered. There was glass everywhere. We had to call in someone to fix it that day, before the performance started.” He motioned to one of the heavy and old wood-and-glass doors behind her.

“So he was angry. And he stormed out . . .” Diana mused, thoughtful. This was looking better and better. “Did he say anything?”

“Oh, yes. I’ll never forget. He made a big scene. He was calling Huber a phony, a charlatan, a second-rate rock-star performer with no real talent. That sort of thing. It was definitely a show.” He grinned. “I suppose one would do that, after they’d just been sacked.”

“You wouldn’t happen to know where Graf lives, would you?”

“No, but it’s probably still in our records,” he said, pulling away from the window and starting to type on the computer. He squinted at the screen. “Here it is. It’s—”

He looked up and stopped, then sheepishly looked around.

Then he shook his head. “I probably shouldn’t tell you this. I’m in enough trouble for letting you in to check the lost and found.”

“Dieter. You said I was too grandmotherly to be a murderer. Don’t you want to help find out who could’ve done this terrible thing?” she coaxed, leaning forward to see if she could glimpse the address on her own.

“Well, yeah . . . it makes sense . . . and I bet you could probably find his address online, anyway.” Finally, he reached down, scribbled something on a piece of paper, and handed it to her. He looked over his shoulder again. “But you didn’t get it here. Got it?”

She took the paper and held it up triumphantly. “Yes. Of course! Thank you.”

Quickly stepping outside, she looked at the address on the paper. *Ybbsstrasse 97. Good luck pronouncing that one.*

She started to enter it into her GPS but frowned when she saw that it was in a location on the other side of town. She was far too tired, after all her gallivanting, to walk it. She marched to the corner and lifted a hand, hailing a taxi.

When she slid into the back of the cab, a message popped up from her youngest, Bea: *OMG you will never believe what Hai just told me!*

She typed in: *What?* expecting something big, like that a tsunami was on its way or foreign invaders were storming Austria.

Then she looked up and realized the driver was still waiting there, with the meter running, for directions. "Oh. Uh. Ninety-seven, yibber—yib . . ." She finally gave up and handed him the paper. "Sorry."

The driver nodded and headed off. By then, she had another message from Bea: *He tells me he wants to have sushi at the wedding. As a main course!*

Diana stared at it, failing to see the problem. *So?*

So? It's absolutely gross. That's why.

She typed in: *Not everyone thinks so.*

Bea's response: *But I do! Doesn't what I think count? Like I want to start my rest of forever eating slimy raw fish.*

Diana typed in: *Bea, honey, don't get carried away. You're going to be with the man of your dreams for the rest of your lives. That's all that matters.*

A second later, her phone started to ring. She answered, already knowing what to expect from her young daughter.

"Mom!" she sing-songed the second Diana brought the phone to her ear. "How can you say that's all that matters? A wedding is a very important day. Practically, the most important day in my life!"

"Well, is the sushi going to ruin it? Honey. I really can't talk. I have—"

"Mom, you don't get it. My entire life is hanging in the balance as we speak," she said, as if she was explaining a difficult concept to a toddler. "Of course it matters. But it's not all that matters. Yes, Hai and I love each other and want to build a life together. But there's nothing wrong with having everything just so—in fact, it's important to begin things in a good way! And sushi will traumatize me."

Diana glanced out the window, as the buildings of Vienna blurred by. There was a beautiful columned building flying an Austrian flag and a statue of some Greek goddess in gold—but she missed it. Maybe she could check it out on the way back. "Funny. Your father and I had a wedding that was less than perfect. We got marr—"

"I know, I know. The local church, with a reception at the VFW Hall next door. But mom, things are different now. That was a simpler time. You don't elope and spend the weekend in Niagara Falls for your honeymoon anymore. That ship has sailed."

"*My* parents did the Niagara Falls thing," Diana corrected. "We did Bermuda. But any way it's done, it doesn't matter. It's still all about the love. The commitment. Not what kind of food is served. But like I said, I have to go. I'm in the--"

"Mom. Come on. This is important."

"And my life isn't?"

"Your life is vacationing, mom."

Oh, she doesn't know the half of it. "Why is it not important to you that I have a good time on my vacation?"

Bea groaned. Her youngest always had been one for exaggerated emotions and drama. "Yeah. It is. Great. You can tell me all about the latest museum you went to, later. But what do you think I should tell Hai? I mean, I'm the bride. Is it bad to put my foot down?"

"No," she said, as the taxi began to slow in a rather unkempt part of town on the outskirts of the city. Gone were the massive, architectural marvels that had defined the center of the city; now, there were small, narrow, nondescript townhomes in a dingy gray, lined like soldiers, shoulder-to-shoulder up the street. "But you choose your battles, dear."

"Is that all you have to say?" Bea said, clicking her tongue. "Mom. Sometimes I get the feeling you really don't even care about us!"

Diana had been gazing up at the home that the taxi had stopped in front of. She looked at the driver with a question on her face; he motioned to the place and nodded. She ran her credit card through and glanced up at the place. As she did, she was hit with an obsessive need to end the call and get a move on. Strange, since she always loved hearing from her kids. But lately, their constant messaging had driven her nearly to the brink. And now, the investigation needed her.

"Mom! Hello?" her daughter groused, impatient.

Diana scrambled out of the car and slammed the door, this time, being sure that she didn't catch any part of her clothing in it. Her face was steaming by the time she stepped onto the curb. She thought about the last item she'd written on her itinerary: *Stand up for yourself!*

Her head was spinning. She pressed her lips together like a volcano ready to blow its top. *Come on Diana. It's now or never.*

"Listen to me, young lady," she said, in the voice she'd used when Bea was five and spilled chocolate milk all over the living room rug. "I may be your mother, but I am not your slave! I am not at your beck and call, waiting to solve all your problems. I have enough of my own problems than to worry about solving everyone else's, too! I thought I raised you to be someone with the wisdom to make her own way in the world! Now, don't tell me that isn't true!"

She realized she was shouting into the phone when a woman who was walking on the sidewalk crossed to the other side of the street to avoid her.

"Mom," Bea said quietly, sufficiently reprimanded. For a second, Diana felt guilty, like she had when her daughter had wanted to play but she was too busy with work. Her face heated and her temples pounded. "What is up with you?"

Diana took a deep breath and let it out. It was the stress, mostly, of yet another murder investigation. But after how up-in-arms they'd gotten over the last one, she didn't want to tell them about it. Not to mention that Bea, Agatha Christie fanatic that she was, would probably hop the next plane to Vienna, just so she could help solve it.

Calm down, Diana. Breathe.

The next time she spoke, her voice was more in controlled. "Nothing. Nothing at all. I'm sorry if I was abrupt. I just want to know that my daughter is equipped to handle things. Especially small things, like this."

"It's not—"

"No one is bleeding or dying. It's small."

She was silent for a moment. Then she said, "Well, yes, in those terms, it is. But a girl only gets married once. At least, I hope. And geez. Most moms would love to help their daughters plan their weddings."

"And I will, my love. I promise. But these decisions are not mine to make. They're yours and your husband-to-be's. Communicate. Work things out together. That's what marriage is all about."

She sighed. "I guess. All right. Fine. I suppose I'll talk it over with him. Maybe we can compromise and have it during the cocktail hour."

"Good, that's the spirit." She looked up at the townhome. The windows were covered in shades, leaking nothing of what was inside. She wondered if Gunther Graf had completely self-destructed after his firing, and now lived in utter darkness and despair. *Only one way to find out.* "I have to go."

When she got to the foot of the stairs, she noticed a small sign in the window: *Musikunterricht,* with a phone number underneath.

I don't know what that means, but it has to have something to do with Music. And that means I'm probably in the right place. Of course, just about everything in this city has to do with music. . .

"All right, Mommy. Have fun."

She ended the call and stuffed the phone back into her purse. No, this probably wouldn't be fun, but it would be necessary. She needed to move the investigation along, and she was sure that Gunther Graf, former lead pianist of the Vienna Philharmonic, held the key.

CHAPTER NINETEEN

Diana gripped the iron handle and pulled herself up the steps, hoping and praying that this would be the answer to all her questions. When she reached the top of the landing, she looked up and down the street, shuddering at the thought of those two scary lawmen, Moser and Ugbodu. They weren't happy before. They'd go practically ballistic if they saw her, now.

She pressed on the doorbell and heard a faint buzzing inside. A moment later, an entirely bald, very tall man with a trim white beard answered the door. He had watery blue eyes and despite his relative lankiness, a bit of a double chin under his whiskers. He was wearing a cardigan over a dress shirt and slacks, with slippers. *What a very Mr. Rogers ensemble,* Diana thought.

That didn't mean she suspected him any less.

"Hello," she said. "Mr. Graf?"

He smiled. "That is correct. Are you looking for lessons for yourself or someone else?" His voice was as gentle and sweet as Mr. Roger's, too, with only a slight German accent.

She patted her chest. "Oh no. Oh no no. I'm not looking for lessons. You see, I've come from *Musikverein,* and—"

He smiled broadly. "A-ha. I knew you'd be coming around. I thought it might take a bit longer, but once I read the news about that charlatan, I suspected it would not be long before you came knocking on my door."

She stared at him in confusion.

"Here are my demands. I want the big dressing room. Not that little closet you thought fit to put me in, before. Also, I don't think it's too much to ask for every third Friday off. I have grandchildren, now. And—"

"Oh. No. Actually, I'm not *from Musikverein.* I just walked over here from there."

He frowned. "You aren't part of the board?"

She shook her head.

He punched the air weakly. "Rats. I thought you were. I was going to have a lot of fun at your expense. Dangle you in the wind for hours and days and weeks, waiting for my response as to whether I'd return. Nothing personal, you see. Just, after their treatment of me, they deserve it, you see."

Diana nodded. "I understand. I am sure they'll be asking you back soon. I hear you're quite a talent."

"That's right. I am. Better than that charlatan, that's for certain, though I hate to speak ill of the dead." He shook his head. "It's a shame he's dead. Don't get me wrong. I wouldn't wish death on anyone. But his technique was atrocious. So cold. So clinical and unfeeling. I often thought he must've been taught by a computer!"

That sounded similar to what his niece had said at the Opus café. "So you two didn't get along?"

He snorted. "We're night and day. But those idiots couldn't see. Didn't care. Only cared about ticket sales. So they put the show monkey in front, to bring the crowds," Gunther said, shaking his head. Then he tilted his head and his eyes met hers. "I'm sure you didn't come here to discuss my gripes with the Philharmonic, though? And you didn't come for a lesson? So what are you here for?"

It was rare for Diana to meet someone so friendly to strangers and willing to talk to them. It might have been the Mr. Rogers association, but Gunther Graf had an easy, likable manner about him, a bit like a dotty old grandfather. Still, she knew looks could be deceiving. "Well . . . have the police been to see you?"

He nodded slightly. "Yes. Briefly."

"Oh." *But maybe there is some information the police might have missed, if they were only here briefly.* "I suppose you can say that I'm invested in the murder, since I found the body."

His eyes widened. "You did?"

"Yes. I attended the last performance and then went in back to get my program signed. That's when I found him. So naturally, I'm a suspect."

He waved her in. "Well, that's interesting. Come in, come in. I want to hear all about it. Would you like some tea?"

"Well, sure, thank you," she said, following him into a bright home with very high ceilings. In the long hallway, she passed a living room with floor-to-ceiling bookcases, and another room, with nothing but a massive grand piano. The white kitchen at the back of the house was tidy and filled with sun. She peered around at the place, trying to find any detail that might point to him as a murderer. But there wasn't much. It was a neat, well-appointed home, with likely expensive, antique but understated furnishings. If Graf had a motive, it probably wasn't financial.

He directed her to sit at a little table and began fussing with the teapot, filling it under the faucet and setting it to boil. A moment later, he had a tray with all the tea fixings, along with little cookies, which suggested he had tea often with others.

"You live here alone?" she asked him.

"Very much so. My wife passed three years ago, bless her soul."

"Was she a musician, too?"

"Oh, no. But she had an appreciation for it. In fact, we met in *Musikverein,* years ago, after one of my performances. So you're American, eh? Been to our *Musikverein*? What did you think?"

"I loved it. It's so much more beautiful than what I saw on television. Being there was like a dream," she gushed. "It must be lovely to play there?"

"Lovely? Oh. You know, the performer is only part of the equation. The music, the accompaniment, play parts, but the locale is crucial. And *Musikverein* is like . . . like coming home." His eyes seemed to get wet as he mused about the place. Diana could tell he missed it. "I play my stuff here every day, and eh. It's missing something. Nothing sounds as good as it does there, in that golden hall. It elevates the music to the heavens. There is nowhere else in the world where I'd rather play."

She let out a sigh. "It's such a shame that you can't."

He shrugged. The kettle began to whistle. He took it off the stove and poured it into two dainty blue teacups. Diana helped herself to sugar cubes and cream.

"When did you meet Lukas Huber?"

He settled himself into a chair and groaned. "Probably just after that. Arrogant little man."

"So you didn't like him from the start?"

He shook his head. "I can't say I did. You know, he actually accused me of being messy? He's the one who plays like some robot, with no feeling or emotion at all. Technically, he's excellent, but there's no *feeling* there."

Hmm. I wonder if that's why I wasn't moved to tears. "I think I know what you mean," she said, sipping her tea. She swallowed and said, "Sounds like it was a bit of a Mozart-Salieri relationship?"

"I wouldn't say that. First, I am not a composer. Not in the least. Never had those sorts of aspirations—the *playing* was my gift, my talent, and I pushed it to the greatest extent I could. And secondly, that relationship is built on a lot of conjecture. There's enough evidence to suggest that the two composers had more of a mutual admiration for one another, rather than an out-and-out, bitter rivalry."

"Is that so?"

"Hmm. Yes. Salieri taught Mozart's son. Did you know that?"

"No . . . I didn't."

"They may have enjoyed a bit of fun at each other's expense, and I don't doubt there was envy, but I think it all stemmed from their appreciation of each other's talents." He placed his teacup down and gazed at it sourly. "I had no such admiration for Huber. He was a cheat, a scoundrel, a flake, and a talentless hack, through and through. Jealous? How can one be jealous of a snake?"

Diana's jaw dropped. She knew he disliked the man, but it was only then that she saw how absolutely disgusted Graf was by him.

He laughed. "In case there should ever be any doubt upon where I stand."

"My. I see that," Diana said. She could almost feel the hate radiating off of him.

He leaned forward and rubbed his hands together. "So you must tell me. How was he found?"

"He was lying on the floor of his dressing room. I accidentally stepped on his hand when I went in. I believe he'd been strangled by his neck-tie."

"Ah. Interesting." For someone who didn't want the man dead, he certainly had a lot of interest. "But not exactly unanticipated. He lived his life wildly. All those women, all those insults he hurled about. Arrogant piss-ant. I always knew he'd piss off the wrong person one day."

"I guess he did. Do you have any idea who could've done it?"

He shrugged. "Probably one of the husbands of the women he wooed, or some sort of thing," he said, pushing a plate of star-shaped shortbread over to her. "He didn't care much for the institution of marriage, I could tell. Have a cookie. I bake them myself."

She took one and nibbled it. "Were you there, the night of the performance?"

He scoffed. "Me? No. I'd be sooner entertained by a cup of nails, rattling around in a clothes dryer. His own composition. Ha! He stole a good part of it from Liszt."

Diana's ears perked up. "So you heard it before?" she asked, confused. Hadn't she read that that was the first time it was being performed?

"No. I didn't need to. He steals everything from Liszt. Twists it around and makes it sound slightly different, but a musician's ear can *untwist* it." He eyed her carefully. "Oh, Dear. I know what you're thinking. And you are barking up the wrong tree, I'm afraid. The thing is, everyone in that hall—every worker, usher, ticket-taker, and musician—knows me. There's no way I could've been anywhere near that hall without someone recognizing me."

She nodded, as she was just coming to the same conclusion herself. He was a larger man, someone people would notice. Plus, he was older, and a bit slower, too. He didn't exactly seem like the type to be sneaky or underhanded at all. "I see."

"So I'm afraid if you came here to accuse me of murder, you're wasting your time."

She tittered. "Oh, no, I wasn't doing that. But I was interested in knowing your interpretation—as a piano virtuoso—of his music."

"Trash. It's well-known. The good parts are Liszt. And then the bits of original composition he adds are simply fluff. Terrible." He chewed on a cookie, shortbread crumbs catching in his white beard. "It pains me to see the hallowed halls of the great place tainted by his output. I don't understand in the least why he wasn't laughed off the stage for it."

"It was all right," Diana said.

"All right? My condolences to your ears." He laughed. "But I suppose it was my outright abhorrence of his work that wound up getting me sacked."

"Is that right?"

He nodded. "Oh, he was always going to be their principal player. I think he might've wooed a couple of the women on the board, and he was the talk of Vienna. But they might have kept me on to fill in for him, if necessary, had I not been so outspoken about my hate for him." He shrugged. "I couldn't help it. I suppose that's why the police came knocking on my door, like you. But besides agreeing that I'd have been recognized if I went near the place, I was also out of town last night, in *Hallstatt,* visiting friends. I gave their names to the police, but I'm more than happy to give them to you, as well, if you'd like to check?"

She wiped her mouth with her napkin and shook her head. She believed him. "That's not necessary. So . . . do you think you will go back to the Vienna Philharmonic, if they ask you?"

"No," he said, to her surprise.

"Really?"

He shrugged. "What can I say. I'm an older man, and as much as I love to play, the rigors of the Philharmonic were exhausting. Performing Mozart takes a lot out of you. I enjoy teaching little children how to play much more. They come to my house and their smiles are bright and they love to learn. And I have grandchildren now, too! Yes, I suppose you can say I'm happy with the life I have now, and I've made my peace with Lukas Huber, God rest his soul."

"Oh. That's great. I am glad to hear it." Diana forced a smile, even though inside, her hopes were plummeting. If Gunther Graf wasn't a suspect . . . that brought her right to square one. Again.

She stood up and checked her phone. "Thank you, but I have to be going. I would've loved to hear you play."

"Well, my door is always open, Miss . . ." he frowned. "I didn't get your name?"

"Diana," she said, shaking his head. "Diana St. James. It's very nice to meet you."

"Likewise. Please, do stop in, whenever you would like. I'd love to play for you."

She smiled as she left, wishing she could take him up on that offer. Maybe the lack of emotion in Huber's playing was what had stunted her before.

But now, she felt like she was running out of time. The police were already ahead of her, and if they didn't find any other suspects, the target would wind up, drilled right into her back. She had to think. Who else could have done this?

CHAPTER TWENTY

As Diana wandered back toward the hotel, she came to the columned building she'd seen earlier. Checking her map, she realized it was the Austrian parliament building. The statue in front of it was Pallas Athene, a several-meters-tall representation of the goddess, adorned in a golden wreath. Several other real and mythological figures sat at her feet, but it was the majestic and graceful goddess that Diana stared at, now.

"You are the goddess of wisdom. I'd certainly like some of that now. What should I do?" she asked.

Similar to Brahms and Mozart, she wasn't saying much.

I really do need to stop talking to these statues before Moser comes and carts me off to the looney bin.

Diana walked to a bench and sat down, gazing at it. The sun was setting behind it, giving it an otherworldly aura. All day had been spent running around, looking for clues to Huber's murder, but she'd made little headway. She hadn't even really seen much of the city's landmarks. The day had been a bust.

The only thing she did know was that her feet hurt. It probably wasn't a good idea to attempt a walk back to the hotel. She needed to hail a cab.

Grabbing her phone, she looked at the display, thinking she'd see more messages from the family. But other than a few push notifications for her different apps—a blowout sale on rugs at the local department store, Breaking News of something the governor did back in New York— there was nothing.

She stared at it, wondering if her phone was even working. *What happened to them? Are my messages going through?*

She went to her "settings" panel and toggled in and out of Airplane Mode, then went to her other messages, to make sure she hadn't missed anything.

But there was nothing.

Remembering back to her conversation with Bea, she wondered if that was the reason. By now, Bea had probably told Evan and Lily about how she'd gone off the deep end and jumped down Bea's throat. They were all probably scared to contact her, considering how she'd cut all of them off. Lily had probably told them about the murder, by now, too. Now, they'd all decided to give up on her, to leave her to deal with her own situation . . . just like she'd told all of them to do.

She missed them. And of course, now, when she really wanted someone to talk to, she was alone.

Diana's back straightened against the wooden bench. Near Pallas Athene, a man with an accordion was playing, a slow, mournful song. It was sad, but by now, Diana knew it wouldn't move her to tears. Maybe nothing ever would, again.

The thought irritated her. It was her own fault, wanting more out of this trip then just some tourist traps that anyone could see. She wanted things that might have been truly impossible. Falling in love in Italy? No, that hadn't happened, but she'd fallen in love *with* Italy. She'd told herself that was good enough.

But was it? Had she gone past that part of her life, where falling in love mattered? And would she be satisfied, just hearing beautiful music that didn't move her to tears? Was she so closed off now, so jaded, that things didn't impress upon her that way?

Maybe. Maybe she should have just accepted that she couldn't have what she wanted. It should have been easy. After all, a million years ago, she'd been in love with Stephane, that gorgeous Frenchman. And it'd fallen apart, leaving her to marry Evan.

Her life had been all about changed plans, about making do with not-quite-perfect.

Maybe she should've just accepted that some things were impossible.

Feeling especially low, she went to the curb and hailed a cab. As she slid into the back and directed the driver to take her back to the Hotel Beethoven, she looked out and wondered if the same held true for this murder. Maybe her trying to solve it was impossible. Maybe she should just let the police do their work and come to their own conclusions, and hope that that conclusion didn't point to her as the killer.

When the cab pulled up to the front of the hotel, she paid the driver and stepped out, wondering what to do for dinner. *There was a little restaurant downstairs, on the corner,* she thought, scanning the area to find it. *Or maybe better yet, room service. The last thing I want to do is go somewhere and run into Hans.*

Actually, sadly, she'd have liked to talk to Hans, at that moment. At least he wouldn't have been questioning her about the murder.

As she scanned the area, her eyes landed on a man, standing behind a potted bush at the entrance. There was no mistaking him, even through all that foliage. Ugbodu. Perhaps he was trying to be inconspicuous, but a dark-skinned man of African descent didn't exactly do inconspicuous in a place like Austria. Was he . . . following her?

Of course he is, Diana. You've been directly associated with three murders in Europe so far. What do you expect?

The second he noticed her watching, he quickly lowered his sunglasses and pretended to be very interested in the brochure he was holding.

She waved at him.

He turned away and started briskly walking up the block, disappearing around a corner.

Well, that settles it, then. Room service.

She stepped into the small lobby, shoulders slumped. Here, she should've been enjoying Vienna for all it was worth, and now, once more, she was relegated to a hotel room, and room service, to avoid the prying eyes of the police. As she walked toward the reception desk, she felt like the staff was looking at her, like they thought she was guilty, too. Maybe somehow everyone knew?

She jabbed on the elevator button and when it opened, and was empty, she sighed with relief as she scuttled in.

The first thing she saw when the doors closed was a framed picture of *Musikverein.*

She stared at it closely. *Oh, hello. Why did I never notice you before?*

Though the subject of bad memories, the place still made her pulse skitter with delight. It had such a history that one bad thing, even a murder, couldn't erase it. And Gunther Graf had spoken with such love about the place and the music he'd made there. She felt love, herself, for it, and she wasn't a musician. She could only imagine how close to the place the actual performers were. They must've—

Suddenly, she stopped, as a thought hit her, right between the eyes.

The elevator dinged, and the doors began to open.

But instead of going out, she jabbed the door closed button hard, and pressed the button for the lobby. Why hadn't she thought of it before? She couldn't go to her room just yet. Not until she checked something out.

As soon as the doors slid open, she exploded out into the lobby, and came face to face with . . . Marius Ugbodu.

"Oh!" she breathed in surprise, then realized she was stepping on his toes. She backed away as if her feet had been on hot coals.

He stared at her, stone-faced. "Where are you going?"

"Just to get some fresh air, you know?" she said, pointing for the doors. "What are you doing here?"

"This is my hotel," he said.

She squinted, flustered. "You own it?"

He looked at her, with an expression that said, *Are all Americans this idiotic?* "I'm staying here."

"Oh. I see. That's nice." She tried to step aside. "Then sleep tight! Have a good--"

"Ms. St. James?" he asked, that low timbre making her knees knock together.

"Yes?"

"You're acting very oddly. Where are you going?" he repeated, this time, in a serious, *Don't mess with me* voice.

Her heart stopped. Her blood ran cold. She took a step away and tried to calm her breathing. "Like I said. Just a walk. I was going to call it a day from my sightseeing, but it seems a shame to stay in when it's such a beautiful night out. Are you attempting to follow me, Mr. Ugbodu?"

His features softened the tiniest bit, and he shook his head a little. "No. Have a good night."

She spun on her heel and headed for the door, trying to walk at a leisurely pace, so she wouldn't arouse suspicion. When she stepped outside and looked over her shoulder to confirm he wasn't following her, she began to walk at a brisk pace, not quite running, but close.

She simply had to get to *Musikverein* before it closed for the night.

CHAPTER TWENTY ONE

She practically raced back to the music hall, thinking about the possibilities. Yes, it made sense that whoever killed Huber must've been someone who could easily slip backstage. Someone who belonged there, like a worker or performer.

But when she returned to *Musikverein*, she wasn't alone.

No, the streets outside the building were crowded with people, clustered together, standing still and waving signs. At first, Diana thought it was some kind of protest. But as she neared it, she noticed the candles, the crying women, and the flowers. All of the posters were taken from Lukas Huber's audio recordings. It was a vigil for their beloved artist, snatched from the world in the prime of his life. There were a few police cars nearby, and even some television crews.

Diana wove her way through the many tightly packed bodies, listening to the weeping and moaning. Cheeks everywhere were wet, eyes red, just like Pia's and Nina's had been. At one point, a woman let out a heart-wrenching sob, fisted both hands, and cried out to the heavens in German. Diana assumed it was something like, "Why, God? Why?"

At the steps to the music hall, she could go no farther. A police officer was standing there, looking rather uncomfortable. She looked over at the people around her. The vigil might have been peaceful for now, but emotions were running high. One of the women, a young blonde, said, "You! Police officer! Why have you not caught his murderer yet?"

"Whoever did this should die!" another person shouted.

The police officer, who couldn't have been any older than Bea, cleared his throat. "We're doing everything we can," he said, voice cracking. "It just happened last night. These things take—"

"Do more! The killer is out there, running loose! And you're here, doing nothing!" a curly-haired, matronly woman shouted at him.

"*Ja!*" another person shouted, holding up a fist.

Give him a break. He is trying to keep the peace and stop the music hall from being overtaken by you crazed fans, she thought, trying to give him an encouraging smile. He wasn't looking at her, though.

His eyes were focused on the woman in front of him, who was in the process of spitting on his feet. She turned and punched her hand in the air and started a rallying cry. "Find the killer! Find the killer!"

The officer started to back away as everyone around Diana began to repeat the slogan. The vigil wasn't a vigil anymore—these people were getting as rowdy as they'd been as fans, in the back of the music hall, when Huber had been alive. More police officers were arriving, much to the young officer's relief. Diana looked around for a way to slip inside but found none. *And I'm not going to find one this way,* she thought. *I need to go around back.*

Rabid Huber fans elbowed her as she struggled to make her way out from the protest, moving herself parallel to the blockades. When she emerged from the crowd, she took a deep breath and scanned the area, expecting to see Detective Moser with the other officers, or Ugbodu watching her from behind a tree in the park across the street. No. He hadn't followed her.

The police had enough on their hands, watching the crowd to make sure it didn't get out of order. Skirting around the police cars, Diana walked quickly toward the box office at the back of the building. There were far fewer people there, as most everyone had been drawn to the chaos happening at the front of the building.

She crossed the street and was just about to open the door to the box office when it opened on its own, and Sheila, the young ticket-taker that worked with Dieter, came out. She stopped short. "You're back," she mumbled, eyeing her suspiciously. "Looking for your *stole* again?"

"Yes, I am. But no--"

"Good. Because we all know that was a big lie."

Oh, no, Diana. She's onto you. Think quick. "Actually, this time I came to see about purchasing some—"

"I told you, no ticket sales today. We all know why you were here, anyway. It's why all those women were here. They all want a piece of the great Lukas Huber. Do you know how many times we've heard of women breaking into his dressing room to get a memento of his?" She rolled her eyes. "It's exhausting. And now, it's even worse, that he's dead. And security is absolutely worthless."

"People have been breaking into his dressing room?"

She nodded. "Haven't you seen the pictures posted online? Someone got in there and took a bunch of photos."

"No, I must've—"

She checked her phone. "I've got to go. I've got somewhere to be."

"I promise, I wasn't here to steal from his dressing room. I was just wondering . . . Is it too late to buy tickets for an upcoming performance?"

She frowned. "We told you. Ticket sales were suspended for now. Besides, we just closed."

"Yes, but I'm leaving town soon," she said, thinking quickly. "And I was wondering if I couldn't put my name on the list to get into the New Year's Concert?"

"That's a lottery," she said. "It's pretty hard to get those tickets."

"I know, but—"

"Dieter's inside, closing up. You can ask to add your name to the lottery. He'll do it for you." She hurried down the steps without another word.

Diana turned to the double doors. *Perfect.*

Looking over her shoulder once to make sure no one was watching her, she hurried inside, expecting to see Dieter's face behind the box office window. But the space was empty. The inside of the box office was dark. "Hello?" she called out, but there was no response.

Even more perfect.

She went past the box office, through the open double doors, toward the main lobby. The place was just as empty as it had been the night she'd returned to apologize to Lukas Huber. She shivered at the recollection. Now, though, there was no clean-up crew, the bar was closed, and everything looked spotless and untouched. She crossed the lobby, her feet making no noise on the lush carpeting, and went to the curtain.

Pulling it aside, she found the same empty hallway she'd travelled before. At the end of it, she came to the spot where she'd seen Lukas Huber, surrounded by his admirers. This area was empty as well, and darker, lit only by a few emergency floodlights above. She quickly made her way to the hallway with Huber's dressing room. When she stopped outside it, she noted that there was no tape, nothing to indicate it was a crime scene at all.

She took a deep breath and pushed open the door.

There, on the floor, she almost expected to see a body, sprawled, just as it had been on that fateful night. But the carpet looked as it had recently been vacuumed. In fact, as she looked around, she realized that the dressing room had been cleared out. Already.

No, that's not possible. Unless the women sneaked in and stole all his personal items away.

She found the light switch and flipped it on. Sure enough, the vanity where his many cards and gifts from admirers was now clear. That big stack of press photos was gone, too; she had to imagine the two in her purse would probably be worth a lot more, now. Every surface had once been covered with little mementos from his many fans, but now, they were all gone. Carefully, she crossed to the vanity and opened some of the drawers, but they were empty, too.

Maybe the police had removed all of his personal belongings as evidence? Or had the staff removed it all to avoid people sneaking in, hoping to get some souvenir of the famous composer? Whatever the reason, one thing was clear: If Diana was hoping to get some evidence to point to the murderer, she was too late.

Sighing, she turned around and headed back outside, into the hallway. And that was when she heard it.

It was Liszt's Hungarian Rhapsody No. 2, the stirring piano notes wafting down the hallway.

Curious, she moved forward, wondering if it was just a recording, being piped in through speakers, somewhere. But as she neared the back door to the stage, it became clearer. No, someone was playing it live, and in a fast tempo, faster than she'd ever heard it.

She quietly crept to the doorway leading to the darkened stage and peered out. There was the entire shoebox-shaped room, darkened in a way she'd never seen it, so that all of the beautiful details and golden scrollwork were barely visible. There was a dim light at the piano, focused on the keys. The figure seated at the bench was a man possessed, his fingers flying over the keys in a blur. He moved to the music, as if taken away by it, as if his hands were no longer his own but controlled by a higher power. The halls of *Musikverein* made almost any music sound good, but this would've sounded incredible, played anywhere. The music and technique were flawless.

When he finally played the last note, he pulled away from the piano, his chest heaving, and smiled.

Diana strained to see his face and let out a small gasp of surprise.

It was Dieter, the young man from the box office.

CHAPTER TWENTY TWO

He looked up, his eyes locking on hers. He mumbled a curse under his breath.

"Why? I've never seen anyone play Liszt like that."

He shook his head and quickly stood up. "This piano is worth a fortune. If anyone found me here, they'd fire me. But sometimes, when I'm all alone like tonight . . . I can't resist."

She understood. It was likely any music lover with his kind of talent would feel the same. Being that close to one of the most valuable pianos in the world, in the greatest music hall in the world? How could any musician resist the opportunity to try it out? No, she couldn't blame him at all.

There was a smug smile on his face, mixing with a bit of a five o'clock shadow, making him look more like a full-grown man than the gawky, acne-faced young adult he'd been in the light of day. "So what did you think?"

How could he ask that? It was like asking whether any of Mozart's symphonies were any good. "Wow. You were wonderful," she gushed. "I didn't know . . ."

"I don't go around flaunting it, like some people," he said, rubbing his hands together. When he saw that she wasn't going to run and tattle on him, he sat back down. Then he began to play Bach's Aria from the Goldberg Variations, slowly, in a lilting way that Diana had never heard. "This one's my particular favorite. Deceptively simple, it leaves so much room for interpretation."

Diana nodded as she neared him on the stage. She listened for a moment, not wanting to speak and distract him.

But he was the one to speak first. He did it as he played, which she found remarkable. How could he do both at once? Most virtuosos couldn't, could they? "So, does that mean that your meeting with Gunther Graf didn't turn up anything?"

She shook her head. "Not very much. I feel like I've turned up more, right here. I'm just shocked. You're very good. Did you learn how to play at the university?"

He snorted. "Nope. I'm entirely self-taught. Mostly with YouTube videos. I started pretty young, though. I even compose my own stuff. Impressive, right?"

"Yes. Very."

He played some more, his long fingers effortlessly pounding the keys. Pia Zimmerman would probably have been jealous. "So since Gunther didn't pan out, what's your next step? You came back looking for more evidence, hmm? Snooping around the dressing room for clues?"

"Yes," she admitted. "Not that I found anything."

"Of course you didn't. Police cleared it out this morning, and the administration needs to make room for the next virtuoso. We have a show next weekend. Things move quickly around here."

"I see that. Who is the next principal pianist going to be?"

He shrugged. "Not me. That's all I know. Probably Graf."

"Why not you? I know for a fact that Graf isn't interested. You could—"

"Don't get me wrong. I auditioned a long time ago. Got too nervous and screwed it up. I've been wanting another audition, but they're not really interested in someone who learned everything on his own. I don't have the fancy education. Not only do I crack under pressure, but I don't have any formal training. Plus, they say I'm not "flashy" enough. They need another Lang Lang type."

"Well, I love Lang Lang."

He smiled. "Yeah. I do, too. He might be flashy, but he has the talent, at least. You know, it was here, many years ago, I first saw him play. My grandfather took me to the concert. I watched him play Prokofiev's War Sonata #7, and I knew that was what I wanted to do. I told you, I dreamed of being here one day. But not as an usher. On this stage. Playing with the greatest orchestra on earth, in the greatest city on Earth."

"You could be. One day? You're very good."

He shrugged. "Not any day soon." He frowned. "So I guess you're at a dead end. With the murder, I mean?"

Suddenly, without her realizing it, he'd switched over to Schubert's Impromptu Op. 90. How did that happen? His music was hypnotizing, in a way, and yes . . . even more emotional than Huber's had been. For a moment, she could almost imagine shedding a tear . . .

"You all right?"

"Yes. Sorry. The music just captivated me." She laughed. "Actually, I'm not quite at a dead end yet. Meeting with Gunther did get me thinking . . . And I think you might be able to help me, if you're willing."

He abruptly stopped playing and looked at her. "Again?"

"I know, I know . . . I'm sorry if I'm putting your job in jeopardy."

He shrugged. "I wouldn't worry about that. Sheila and I were talking a lot today, and well . . . we're going out after this. I think she likes me." He wiggled his eyebrows.

"She's your boss, though, right?"

He nodded, grinning. "So, yeah . . .I think I don't have to worry too much about all that. I think she likes that I don't follow the rules. Makes me look tough." He pulled his name plate off his polo shirt. "What did you need help with?"

"I was just thinking about the murderer. While I was with Gunther, he made a good point—people would've noticed him if he'd attempted to sneak in there. So my thought is that it likely had to be someone who could be back there without raising any red flags. A member of the crew, or one of the musicians?"

He nodded. "Or Sheila?" He grinned slyly. "Or maybe even me?"

"Well . . ."

"Yeah, I understand. That makes sense. But it doesn't help narrow it down much. There are over two-hundred members in the Philharmonic. And another hundred crew. Do you want to interview them all?"

She frowned. That was a lot of people. And she couldn't interview them all. How would she track them down, keep details on all of them? Detective Moser would probably be onto her way before she got done with such a gargantuan task. "No, of course not. But I thought, you were there that night. Maybe you had an idea of someone who was acting suspicious?"

"Suspicious? No. I was ushering, going back and forth, so I was dealing with all the guests. I didn't really interact with the musicians. No one in the crew was acting odd, that I know of. Well, Sheila, but she's *always* acting odd. Stuck up and kind of aloof. Come to think of it, that might be because he likes me." He grinned. "What do you think? Do women act like that when they like a man?"

"Sometimes. I suppose they do."

"As for the crew and musicians, the police already interviewed everyone. So I'm sure they're on it." He looked back at the piano and cracked his knuckles. "Now where was I?"

"I'm sorry. I'm disturbing you."

He shook his head. "I can play in my sleep. It's hacks like Huber who need absolute silence to perform. But when I play, everything falls away. Nothing can bother me. He's a diva. A true genius doesn't need conditions to be favorable in order to create. And he doesn't need to stand on the shoulders of giants, either."

Diana thought about what Pia had said. Lukas Huber had fallen in love and hadn't created in five years. So yes, it seemed that he did need favorable conditions to create. But the last part of what Dieter said hung in her mind. She leaned on the side of the piano, but then thought better of it—the piano was probably worth more than her entire 401k—and straightened. "What do you mean? Shoulders of giants?"

"Ha. You didn't notice?" He shook his head and smiled a secret smile at the piano keys. "I'm surprised at you. You seem to be quite an expert on music. But don't worry; even the most trained ears don't seem to notice. Only very few can. Listen." He played a few bars of Liszt. "Sound familiar?"

"Sure. That's Liebestraum No. 3. The *Love Dream.* Liszt."

"Right. Good. But then listen to this."

He played a little more. It sounded like something she'd heard before, but she couldn't place where. "What is that?"

"It's the third movement of Huber's Jupiter Symphony. But it's the same piece as Liebestraum, only in a different key, with variations on tone and a few odd notes, here and there. But it's nearly eighty-percent identical."

Her eyes widened. "Really?"

"And I can show you at least five of his recent pieces and make the comparisons to other works."

"Oh, my gosh. Graf mentioned something like that, too. So when you said he was a fraud, you weren't just saying that? He really is one?"

Dieter nodded. "He used to pick lesser-known works, so the average person wouldn't know. Even the experts don't know, because as a fraud, he's a very good one. But Liebestraum, one of Liszt's greatest works? That took guts."

"You didn't tell anyone?"

"Of course I did. I told the conductor. He said he'd take it under advisement and bring it before the board. I don't think he ever did. Or maybe he did, but nothing ever came of it."

"Why? How is that possible?"

He laughed. "Because Lukas Huber sold tickets. And it was like, the more people complained about him being a fraud, the more fame he got. And he loved it. So they swept it under the rug. It was like he could do no wrong. Like, he probably could've appeared on stage and done nothing but rip an enormous fart, and his throngs would've applauded wildly. Ridiculous, right?"

She laughed. "If you say so. I can't believe it. I can't believe he's made it this far on such lies."

"Well, the world isn't fair, that's for sure. I learned that much. It's why people like me are forced to play in the closet, and men like him get all the fanfare."

"I'm so sorry."

"And you can imagine, a young pianist like me, watching that pompous ass, day in, day out, performing his knock-off junk, getting applause and bows and fame, when there are real musicians, better musicians, who practice for hours and hours and hours on end, are so much more worthy than he is?" His voice got distinctly sharper and more intense, and a little spittle flew from his mouth. When he looked at her, a shock of his dark hair tumbled wildly in his face. "You don't know how long I wanted to wring his little pencil neck. Anyone in my position would. Right?"

Wring his neck.

A wave of fear swept over Diana. She took a step back. "Right," she said softly, something suddenly clicking in place in her mind.

Dieter had clearly been jealous of Lukas Huber.

Dieter had called Lukas Huber a fraud, from the start.

Dieter wanted what Lukas Huber had.

Dieter had been at *Musikverein* on the night in question.

And as an employee of the music hall, Dieter could probably go anywhere he wished without raising suspicion.

He placed his fingers on the piano, ready to play. "I'm not sorry he's dead," he said in a low, bitter voice. "That's for sure."

Suddenly, he began to play Chopin's *Marche Funèbre*, the funeral march, and the notes were like a death knell, reverberating deeply in Diana's very soul.

A chill gripped her, slipping its icy tendrils all the way down her spine. No, maybe she didn't know enough about music to tell a fraud from a talented composer. But she had a good feeling that she was in this great, grand music hall . . . with a killer.

*

Diana stood frozen to the spot, each note reverberating inside her, almost like the seconds of a ticking time bomb. She was trying to decide what to do, but her brain felt useless, rehashing the words he'd said: *I wanted to wring his little neck.* Suddenly rushing out of the place would probably raise suspicions. Dieter was young and spry and would probably catch up with her before she made it to the door.

She'd always wanted to be in the golden halls of *Musikverein.* But die here? That was another thing entirely.

As he played his Chopin, he looked over at her, a sick smile on his face. It was that unsettling smile that stuck in her mind and tangled her gut. She needed to find some way to distract him so she could leave and alert the police, outside. Luckily, because of the "vigil-that-was-more-of-a-protest", she knew exactly where to find them.

As she was trying to formulate an excuse, tinkling notes filled the empty space in between the Chopin.

It was The Entertainer, and it was coming from her purse.

She fished it out. *Good timing. For once.* She stared at the display. It was Evan.

Normally, she'd have let it go to voicemail. She always did, with her ex. But now, she'd never been so happy to have him intruding on her life. As Dieter continued to play, Diana pointed at her phone and headed off the stage. "I have to take this."

She pressed the button to take the call and said, in an exaggeratedly happy voice, "Hi, Evan! So glad to hear from you!"

There was a pause. "Diana? Is that you?"

"Of course it's me."

"Are you drunk?"

It was only when she'd made it to the edge of the stage that she realized the music behind her had stopped. "No, don't be silly," she said. "But I've got to—"

"Listen to me, Love. I've been speaking with Bea and she says that she's worried you might be under a lot of stress. Lily said something about another incident you might be tied up in? So if there's anything you need me to come help with, let me—"

"Evan, I really can't—" she began, her heart in her throat as she turned.

Dieter was standing right behind her. He looked bigger than she remembered, more frightening. "You won't tell," he said, his voice desperate. "Will you?"

She shook her head. "I won't. Of course not." She smiled. *Keep it light, Diana.* "Don't you have that date coming up with Sheil—"

"You're lying." He reached over and plucked the phone from her hand. She could hear Evan calling her name on the other end, but the Dieter pressed a button and disconnected the call. The beautiful hall, where all sounds were elevated, seemed to elevate the sound of her beating heart, making it echo in her ears. "I shouldn't be using that piano. I can get a lot of trouble for that. And this job—this hall—is everything to me. You know that. You love music. You have to know that. You have to know what the music means to me. I can't be taken away from here."

She backed up until she found a wall behind her. She nodded, glancing to the side. The doors were open. She could yell, hoping someone would hear her. But there'd been no one else in the place, before. She could jump off the stage and make a run for it and hope he somehow didn't catch up with her. "I won't tell."

"And I don't believe you. You're just another person who will stand in the way of me getting where I want to be. Like everyone else," he said, biting off each word as he gripped her phone in his hands. He was so close, his spittle hit her face. And the wild look in his eyes told Diana that he was capable of anything. Even another murder.

"Dieter, you're scaring me. I don't know what to say. I promise you, I won't say anything about . . . anything," she said. "Just let me go."

He shook his head. "That's not good eno—"

Before he could finish, she slipped to the side. He tried to grab her, but she shook him loose and broke into a run. She jumped from the stage, clumsily hitting her knee on the ground, but gaining her footing quickly and rushing for the aisle.

"What are you—come back here!" he shouted after her. Footsteps pounded behind her.

He was in pursuit.

She tried to pick up speed, but she hadn't run this far and this fast in ages. She had the new shoes that Tilda had given her in Verona, but they lacked traction and slipped upon the carpeted runner. Reaching for the doors, she propelled herself through them and managed a glance behind her. He was so close, practically on her heels. If she had to stop to open a door, he'd catch up with her.

"Stop!" he called after her.

No way, she thought, pumping her legs as fast as they could go as she headed into the lobby. Of course, no one was there.

Flying past the box office, she reached the door to the outside. When she grabbed the handle, she felt his hand on her shoulder, trying to pull her back. "No!" she screamed, ripping open the door with such force that as she moved aside, it collided with his face.

He let out a groan of pain and cupped his hands around his nose as he stumbled back. It gave her the time to slip out the door. By that time, darkness had fallen, and so frantic was she from the chase that she couldn't make out a single shape in the distance. The sound of crowds chanting, *Find the killer!* were still going on, but sounded as if they were miles away. As she rushed down the steps, to the sidewalk, she heard the door behind her slam closed, and fast footfalls, catching up with her.

"Help!" she cried, wishing she hadn't been able to shake Ugbodu. If she hadn't, he'd be here, and witness to this. "Help!"

But everyone must've been at the rally, because the side street was empty. No one heard her cries. Not a single person came to her aid. She was alone, with a killer on her heels.

CHAPTER TWENTY THREE

Diana ran down the street, toward the front of *Musikverein,* screaming at the top of her lungs. It did little good. Though her voice was loud, the voices of the other mourners were even louder. As she approached them, she saw a police car and ran to it.

But there was no police officer.

She glanced behind her just as Dieter reached over and grabbed her by the fabric of her shirt. She heard it ripping, felt the seams popping as she pulled away, and again, she was on the run. When she reached a corner, she went to cross the street, but a car zoomed past, nearly running over her toes. She stumbled back, right into Dieter's chest. He grabbed her, and as he did, she spied Detective Moser, across the street. "Detective!" she screamed.

He saw her at the same time, and his eyes went wide. Hand on the holstered gun at his hip, he went to cross the street, only to be pushed back by the traffic.

"What are you—" Dieter's grip loosened on her.

She took advantage of that momentary reprieve, bolting off, down the street. She didn't get far before she heard a guttural "oof" behind her. Whirling, she found Detective Moser, pinning Dieter to the ground. Cheek pressed against the cement sidewalk, he moaned, "Not my wrist! Not my arm! Watch my fingers! I need those! Ow!" as the detective wrenched his arm back and cuffed him.

Catching her breath, Diana returned to them as the detective said, "What do you think you were doing, chasing after her? Grabbing her like that?"

"He killed Lukas Huber," she shouted, breathless.

"What? No, I didn't!" he whimpered, his voice muffled by the cement. "I swear, I didn't. I just want to play!"

Diana almost laughed. How could he say that, after everything he'd told her? "You confessed to me," she said.

Detective Moser looked up. "He did?"

"Well, practically." She circled around them as Dieter looked up at her miserably. She noticed her phone lying near his body and stooped to pick it up. As she did, he scowled, and Diana backed away, brushing the dust off her phone display. She had four missed calls from Evan. *I'll call him later.*

"Are you crazy, lady? How can you say that? I didn't say anything like that. I—"

"Did you confess to the murder?" Detective Moser said as he wrenched him upright.

"I *didn't*!" he insisted. Now, he looked less like a man and more like a frightened boy. Just as that thought came to her, he began to sob, and a big tear fell down his cheek. Diana almost felt bad for him.

Moser shrugged. "It doesn't matter. We'll bring you in for assault and iron the rest out from jail."

"I didn't mean to," Dieter moaned. "I just didn't want to get in trouble . . . if I lose my job at the hall . . . it's the only thing I have!"

"I think he may have been jealous of Huber," Diana murmured, avoiding his pleading eyes.

He sniffled. "Yeah! I was jealous. I'll admit it. I'll admit I thought he was a fraud. But you've got the wrong guy. I swear!"

"Then why were you chasing after this woman? You'll have to tell that to the court," the detective said, handing him off to two police officers, who guided him to the back of a police cruiser.

Diana shuddered. She expected to feel relief, but now, she felt nothing but dread. Detective Moser glanced at her. "You all right?"

She nodded as she watched the police car drive away. In the back window, she could just make out the head of Dieter, hanging low, chin to his chest. "Yeah. I guess . . . I have children about his age. It just . . ." She clutched at her heart. "Got me."

He nodded. "Yeah. I have kids that age, too. This generation, huh?"

She didn't know. Truth was, for all the people of her generation complaining about the entitlement and laziness of millennials, she actually liked that generation. Because she liked her kids. And she'd like Dieter, too. She understood how it was to work hard at something, only to have it not be recognized, or taken away by another person who maybe hadn't played by the rules. In short, she felt bad for him.

But murder wasn't the answer. In the end, he had to have known that.

He said, "How did you know?"

"I didn't. I came back here, yes . . . even though you told me not to, because I realized whoever did it was probably someone known by everyone, who could easily slip in and out of the back area without being seen. And then I found him there, playing the piano. He told me how jealous he was of Lukas Huber, said he was a fraud. He wouldn't let me leave. And when I escaped, he chased after me."

Detective Moser's strong square jaw worked as he peered down at her. "So he didn't actually confess to murder?"

She said, "No. I guess not. But I'm sure you would agree, if you saw him. He had this wild look in his eye. And he was talking crazy. He said that years and years of playing and watching Huber, who he believed to be a fraud, getting all those accolades, made him want to wring his neck."

The detective raised an eyebrow. "He said he wanted to wring Huber's neck?"

She nodded.

"All right. But that's not the same as actually doing it. Or confessing to doing it. We all say things like that from time to time, don't we?"

"Well . . ." True. She'd wanted to wring Evan's neck more times than she could count. "I guess. Still. I'm sure. He had the motive, the opportunity, everything. He was an usher, taking tickets, for the performance. So he could've easily slipped in without anyone noticing."

The detective pulled out his pad and paged backwards, then stopped. "His name is Dieter Hausman. Twenty-one. Lived in Vienna all his life. He's been working here since he was sixteen. Said he worked here until nine-thirty, when he took a bus home to his apartment, where he lives alone. Arrived there at ten."

"Ah-ha. Alone. That could be a lie. He has no one to corroborate that, I bet."

"As a matter of fact, he doesn't. The landlady at the apartment building says she was asleep, and they don't have cameras."

"Ah-ha." Diana said. "Just as I thought."

"Not only that, he has a prior arrest."

"Really?"

"Yeah. Breaking and entering when he was fifteen. Which he probably hid in order to get his job at the music hall."

Diana said, "So what will happen to him?"

Moser shrugged. "We're going to question him some more, see if we can get him to confess. If nothing else, he's looking at an assault charge. I'll have you come down to the headquarters so you can make a statement."

"Oh, I don't want to press charges for the attempted assault, if that's all you have him for," she said.

He raised an eyebrow. "What?"

"Well, I—"

"If he's a murderer, then—"

"Yes, but . . . I like him. He might be misguided but he seemed nice. And he's talented."

Moser shook his head. "I don't understand you."

She shrugged, unable to understand herself. All signs seemed to point to Dieter. And yet, once again, something tickled in the back of her mind. It was a feeling she'd had before, of everything not being all right, but she tamped it down. *Don't be silly, Diana. The reason you're feeling that way is because he reminds you of your own kids. You should be happy that you helped to get a violent criminal off the streets.*

But maybe that was it. Dieter Hausman didn't seem violent. Wacky, yes. Obsessed with his music, of course. And though he'd chased after her, he hadn't exactly threatened to harm her. He'd just been really . . . intense. Her life had been in danger, though, hadn't it? He'd wanted to hurt her, though, right?

Now that she looked back at it, she wasn't sure. Maybe he'd just wanted her to promise not to tell anyone about playing the piano. Because music was everything to him. His job, and being close to the music hall he loved, was important to him. Maybe he'd just been desperate about that?

Oh, stop overthinking things, Diana. The murderer has been caught. Case closed.

Detective Moser pointed across the street with his chin, to the chanting fans of Lukas Huber. "Well, I know a couple of thousand women who'll think you're a national hero," he said nonchalantly.

"I really didn't do anything," she said.

"I think those people would beg to differ," he said, closing his pad and stuffing it into his pocket. "Good night, Frau St. James. Oh, and by the way, I suppose you're clear, now. You're free to leave the country, if those were your plans."

"Oh. Thank you." She let out a breath of relief.

He paused. "Were they?"

She shrugged. "Actually, I don't know. I haven't really thought of it." She looked around. Now that she had so much time on her hands, she could do anything. But she'd seen most of what she'd wanted to see. She'd experienced the most beautiful music in the greatest hall on Earth. She'd toured many neighborhoods on her walks through Vienna, and she'd enjoyed the local cuisine. What more could she want? "Where do you think I should go next?"

He thought about it. "Where have you already been? You said Paris and Italy?"

She nodded.

"My family and I vacation in a little place in Spain. Baiona. It is by the beach. If you like the beach?"

She smiled, imagining herself sitting out on a sandy beach, tropical drink in hand, letting the waves lull her to sleep under the warm sun. After a trip like this, running from place to place, that sounded like heaven. "I grew up on an island. Long Island. Of course I like the beach."

"Then that's an idea for you." He nodded. "Safe travels."

He headed off and she stood there for a moment, trying to orient herself with the streets so that she could walk back to her hotel. By now, the cries of *Find the killer!* from the vigil a block away had died down. Maybe the news was spreading that the killer had been caught.

Finding her direction, she headed across the street, this time, taking time to enjoy the sights of Vienna. She stopped at every statue, trying to discern their details in the darkness. She walked along the Wien River and breathed in the air, admiring the way the moonlight danced upon the water's surface. She tried to feel at peace.

But no matter how she tried, she couldn't stop thinking of the way that Dieter Hausman had looked at her when he was being handcuffed. He'd looked sad. Desperate.

Innocent?

Okay, now you're going too far, Diana. Did you even hear a word the detective said? He had a motive. No alibi. Previous arrest record. You couldn't find a more perfect killer, in all of Austria.

Shaking off the feeling that seemed to creep its way into her mind, she hurried back the rest of the way to the Hotel Beethoven. When she arrived, she expected to see Ugbodu waiting for her, behind a potted plant. But he was gone. She was truly free.

And it was time to leave.

In her hotel room, she grabbed her suitcase from the top of the closet and opened up her drawers, readying to fill it. Tomorrow, she'd check out of the Hotel Beethoven, leave the Music City behind, and take a train . . . somewhere. Maybe Spain. Maybe somewhere else. The world was her oyster.

But something about that made her feel sad. When she pulled out her itinerary and stared at the third-to-last item she'd written there for her Austria trip, she realized what it was.

Be moved to tears by beautiful music.

She stared at the words, remembering all the times she'd heard music during this trip. Beautiful music. Moving music. The type of music she'd learned to appreciate from her grandparents, and absolutely loved. It had all been so wonderful, but it hadn't quite done the job.

Of course. It's because you haven't completed your bucket list item.

But maybe that was her own fault. Music was frivolous, like flowers. It existed for no other reason than to be beautiful. She'd had so much disappointment and heartbreak in her life. Maybe it had hardened her so much that music couldn't do that to her anymore?

That was it. It had to have been. There had certainly been nothing wrong with all of that music. If she didn't cry, it was because of her.

Oh, well, she thought. *Maybe it's just not meant to be.*

Then she looked at the next items on her to-do list.

Forgive. Feel the calmness and clarity of letting go and *Stand up for yourself!*

Maybe she needed to stop beating herself up for not behaving in a way that was expected of her. Because really, though she was in her mid-fifties, all of this, this independence, was so new to her. She'd lived so long for others; she'd forgotten how to live for herself. She was the one who'd burdened herself with those unrealistic expectations of the woman she was supposed to be now. Perhaps it was time to shed those beliefs and be happy with who she was.

Maybe the person I need to forgive most is myself.

She picked up her phone and typed in a group text to her family: *I appreciate you checking in with me and wanting me to be a part of your life. I'm sorry if I was short with you, but I'm trying to find myself. Just because I need that space doesn't mean I don't love you all more than words can say.*

A moment later, she received a response from Bea: *Okay, Mommy, I love you, too ☺*

She smiled, then finished packing her things and looked around the room. Maybe there had been no tears from beautiful melodies, but that was okay. It had been wonderful, nonetheless.

It was time to move on.

CHAPTER TWENTY FOUR

In the morning, Diana walked out to the balcony of her room and took one last look as the sun rose over the Wien. She smiled. Yes, forgiving and lowering her expectations for herself was the best thing she could do. Once she'd made that resolution, last night, she'd slept like a baby.

Turning back to her room, the gold-leaf wallpaper catching the morning sun, she couldn't help but be in a bright and shiny mood. Goodbyes were always hard, but this felt like a good thing. A new beginning. Grabbing her bag and hoisting it over her shoulder, she took one last sip of her morning coffee and headed out.

As she emerged from the elevator, she saw a lanky young man, sweeping up in the common area. Immediately, she thought of Dieter Hausman. Young, with his whole life ahead of him. How could he have thrown it away like that by murdering Lukas Huber?

Maybe that was the reason it'd hit her so hard, and why immediately, when he was led away in handcuffs, she'd wanted to go home and hug her own kids. It was so senseless. And he'd been so talented. A prodigy, self-taught, and yet that good? What a waste.

Shaking off the sour thought, she went to the front of the hotel and the valet hailed her a cab. "Did you have a pleasant stay, Ma'am?" the young man said with a smile.

She nodded at him, again thinking of Dieter. *Oh, stop it, Diana. Don't overthink things. He's guilty.*

As she slid into the back of the cab, the driver looked over at her. Once again, it was a young man with acne on his face. His prominent Adam's apple as he looked at her. *"Guten Tag."*

"Guten Tag," she repeated half-heartedly, hand on the door. She almost had the urge to pop out and take the next cab. Why was simply everyone reminding her of Dieter? She sat back and tried to ignore it. Soon, she'd be well on her way to Spain, and all this would be behind her. She hoped, at least. "The train station, please."

The car took off, and Diana prepared herself for her last glimpses of the city of Vienna. Instead of marveling at the architecture and many monuments, her eyes caught on a young man, standing with his skateboard, on the corner. He had dark, floppy hair, falling in his face, much like Dieter.

Diana, stop already.

But by the time she arrived at the train station, she was sure she was going insane. She'd seen about ten different boys that really, looked nothing like the boy she'd accused of murder, and yet, she couldn't help feeling that something was wrong.

As she climbed out of the cab and headed for the station doors, she mentally ran through the details of the case. He'd acted guilty. He'd accosted her. He'd looked insane and out of control. He'd chased after her, screaming at her not to tell. He'd had a motive. He'd had the opportunity. He didn't have an alibi.

What else could she possibly want? *Open and shut case,* she thought. *Even Detective Moser seemed convinced.*

Diana went to the ticket office and stood in the line, still thinking. *But he'd worked at Musikverein since he was sixteen. Lukas Huber had been there for years, too. Why did Dieter choose now to murder him? He could've done it any time before then . . .*

She was startled from her thoughts by someone clearing his throat. She blinked and saw the man at the ticket counter, waiting for her expectantly.

"Oh, I'm sorry. A ticket to Spain."

He rolled his eyes. "Barcelona, Madrid, Seville . . .?"

"Oh, um . . ." She hadn't really thought that far into it. Last night, she'd just settled on Spain, but strangely, she hadn't planned much more than that. It was odd, considering she was someone who'd originally planned everything to the letter, dragging along her massive itinerary. "You know, I don't know."

He motioned for her to move aside. "Come back when you decide."

She stepped away and another customer approached the ticket counter, for a fare to Salzburg. Diana, feeling silly, grabbed her phone and paged through it, looking for a map of Spain. She couldn't remember the name of the town Detective Moser had talked about. It had started with a B, hadn't it?

When the man had gotten his ticket to Salzburg, Diana poked her head in. "Do you know of a town in Spain, on the beach, that starts with a B?"

He stared at her for just long enough for her to feel woefully inadequate. "No."

"Fine. Could I just have a ticket to Barcelona, then?" She'd figure out the connecting train to take, later.

He sighed. "Vienna to Zurich to Barcelona," he said. "That will be ninety-six euros."

She handed over the cash. "Thank you. How long is the trip?"

"Ten hours to Zurich, another ten hours to Barcelona. You are lucky. This ticket is the last one; and the train is already here, leaving in a moment." He pointed behind her. "Right that way."

"All right. Thank you." She scooped up the ticket. As she spun, she saw another kid, who was blonde, and far too young to be Dieter, and yet she thought of him, anyway. *Twenty hours. Plenty of time to wallow in doubt over whether I made a mistake.*

She pressed her lips together, willing the thought away as she headed toward the trains.

For the last time, Diana! You did not make a mistake!

The red bullet train was waiting as she walked onto the concourse, and people were boarding. She showed her ticket to a conductor before she boarded. "Is there assigned seating?"

He nodded and pointed toward the back of the train. "Your seat can be found on the second car. Safe travels."

She headed toward the next car and climbed the steps into the train. Walking down the narrow aisle, she smiled. The trains in Europe were nothing like the ones in New York. There was plenty of room to stretch oneself out in, the chairs were padded and comfortable, there was a large table to set her things down on, and the picture window would provide a lovely view of the scenery for the next twenty-hours. She tried to be enthusiastic and excited about the possibilities, but her thoughts kept sinking into despair.

Come on, Diana. This is why you came to Europe to begin with. You'll feel better when you're looking at the Alps from the train.

Following the portly old man in front of her, she checked the seat numbers as she moved along the aisle, and checked them again, looking for 27A.

Before she even got to it, she knew something was wrong. She counted forward, 23, 24, 25, 26 . . . and frowned.

There was a young, red-headed woman, sitting in her seat, staring dreamily out the window.

Diana stopped in front of her, shifting awkwardly as she let the person behind her pass through. The woman must've sensed her presence, because she blinked and turned to her, a question on her face.

"I'm sorry," Diana said kindly, showing her the ticket. "You appear to be in my seat."

"I don't think so," she said in a very French accent, reaching into her pocket and producing her ticket. "Twenty-seven, *oui*?"

"Yes," Diana said, squinting to see the number on her ticket. "But yours says B. This is A."

The woman's eyes went wide. "It is?" She moved her elbow to reveal the letter. "Oh, *excuse-moi.*"

"Honest mistake!" Diana laughed as she pushed out of her seat and grabbed her things. "Believe me, half the time on this trip, I've been in the wrong place at the wrong time, so I understand!"

The woman laughed, too, as she pushed her bag across the aisle, to the correct seat. "It's totally my fault, you see. I'm not good with details like that. I used to rely on my boyfriend to point me in the right direction. It's my first time travelling alone. It's a wonder I haven't gotten hopelessly lost yet!"

"Oh? You are headed to Zurich, yes?" Diana asked.

She nodded as she collapsed into her seat. "I think I did get on the right train, at least. It has been a long trip, but that much, I'm sure about."

"Good! Just making sure!" Diana laughed. "So you're travelling alone, yes?"

"Oh, yes. First time. Just needed to get away from everyone and everything."

"Me too," Diana said, smiling. Maybe she'd have someone to talk to, at least for the Zurich leg, which would make the trip go by a little faster. "It's daunting though, isn't it? I'm always afraid of forgetting something. You have no one else to rely on but yourself. My ex-husband used to be there to pick up for me if I ever forgot anything. But now, my conscience is constantly tickling me, telling me to look back, in case I left something behind!"

"Yes! I know. I keep doing that, too." The woman shrugged. "But I have to say, travelling alone does have its benefits. You get to see whatever you want, whenever you want to!"

"That's so true. My ex-husband wouldn't have liked to do most of the things I did."

"Right? I love my boyfriend, but he's not interested in looking at museums. I got to tour every museum in town!"

"You must've loved that."

"Oh, I did. It was a wonderful trip. Not to mention, this train is sold out. My boyfriend and I would never have been able to get seats together. But I was able to get this seat, last-minute, when my plans changed. Getting single seats is much easier."

"Sold out, really? I didn't even know," Diana said, glad that she'd made the decision to take the ticket when she did. And that was true. She probably wouldn't have gotten to sit at *Musikverein* if she'd been with someone else. She'd only gotten that coveted seat because that woman, Leonie Winkler, had to cancel because she couldn't find babysitting. What a shame it would've been if she'd had to worry about finding a seat for . . .

Suddenly she straightened. Something about that tickled at her mind.

Leonie Winkler couldn't attend Lukas Huber's performance because she'd been unable to get a sitter. At the time, Diana hadn't thought much about it. She'd assumed she'd be going with a husband. But there'd only been one seat. So . . . had she planned on going alone?

Diana sat back, thinking. Certainly, there were plenty of single mothers in the world. But with her wealth, and how well put-together she was, Diana hadn't doubted that she was an aristocrat. She'd taken for granted that she had a husband, and a successful one, maybe a doctor or a politician. Someone who had the influence to secure such a great seat at *Musikverien.*

But a woman like that, not being able to find a sitter? Didn't wealthy women like that have live-in nannies?

Something struck in Diana's mind, something Pia Zimmerman had said: *Every performance, Lukas always has a certain number of seats in the front, set aside. For his many women. But he's never serious about any of them. Usually.*

Also, Diana recollected how distant she'd been about discussing her children. Diana had spoken more about her grown children than Leonie had. It was almost as if . . . as if . . .

As if they didn't exist.

Outside, the conductor was calling for the last few straggling passengers to climb aboard. As he did, another thing Pia has said hit

Diana, straight between the eyes. *He had a definite type, though. Gorgeous. Thin. Big boobs.*

Which described the beautiful Leonie Winkler to a tee. And not only that . . .

She thought of the necklace the woman had been wearing. The amber and silver striped, circular pendant.

Jupiter. Not the god. The planet.

"Oh, my gosh," Diana whispered under her breath, rising to her feet.

"Is everything all right?" the French woman said in concern.

"No," she said, gathering up her things. "But I know a way to fix it. I've got to get off this train!"

She rushed for the door and climbed down the stairs as fast as she could. Rushing across the concourse, she hurried to hail a cab.

CHAPTER TWENTY FIVE

Leonie Winkler. Leonie Winkler. Leonie Winkler.

The name repeated in Diana's head as she stood there, waiting for a cab. The second it pulled up and she slid inside, she cursed herself for being so impulsive. *Diana. Don't be silly. You can't just tell the driver "Take me to Leonie Winkler!"*

"Hello," she said to the driver. "Uh . . . can we just drive around a little? I'm looking for someone and I'm not sure where to find her."

"All right," the driver, an old man, said after a moment, heading off from the curb.

She watched the same sights she'd seen all week, rushing by her in a blur, her mind spiraling through the possibilities.

Suddenly, an idea struck her. *When you've lost something, you always return to the last place you had it.* "Oh! I know. Café Johann Strauss, please."

"Certainly," he said kindly. "First time in the city?"

"Actually . . . I've been here a few days. I was just about to leave, but I forgot something."

"Oh . . ." He seemed perplexed. "I'm assuming what you forgot must be very dear to you, then, if you're in such a rush?"

Diana shook her head. "I think she's a murderer."

"What?" He stared at her a beat too long in the rear-view mirror, so that he nearly rear-ended the car in front of him.

She shook her head and fisted her hands at her sides, willing the cab to go around the traffic. If this hunch was right, then that meant her intuition had been correct. Poor Dieter was innocent. "Forget it. If you could hurry, please?"

"I'll do my best, but the traffic is pretty terrible, this time of day," he said, turning the wheel to go around the slow car and punching the gas. Her head slammed back against the seat back as the car surged forward.

Meanwhile, she jabbed *Leonie Winkler Vienna* into the search bar on her phone. The internet brought up very little. There was a photo of a Leonie Winkler, but she was over ninety, and when Diana tapped on it, she realized it was an obituary. There was nothing about the young, beautiful woman Diana had met in the café. No photograph. No address. Had she used a fake name? Had the whole thing been a ruse?

And if so . . . why?

Then she picked up her phone and called the detective. The phone went right to voicemail. Sighing, the second she heard the beep, she said, "Detective Moser. I had an idea. It's Diana, by the way. I have a feeling Dieter Hausman might be innocent. I'll call you when I know more. Thanks."

The cab pulled up at the front of the hotel that housed the café. She quickly paid the fare and got out, dragging her luggage with her. When she went inside, the place was as empty as it was the first time she'd been there. Diana looked around, hoping that she'd be lucky and find Leonie Winkler, sitting there in the booth, just as she had been the day she met her. But no, the booth was empty. No Leonie.

She went up to the counter, where a bored barista with a goatee was cleaning the coffee machine. He looked up at her and let out a grunt, clearly annoyed that she was interrupting his duties. "*Ja*?"

"Hi. I wonder if you could help me? I'm looking for a woman?"

He rolled his eyes and wiped his hands on a dirty dish rag. "Aren't we all?"

Diana ignored his attempt at wittiness. "She was here a couple days ago. I thought maybe she frequents the place? Probably mid-thirties, dark hair, thin, very made-up, but pretty. Dresses very elegantly. You'd notice her."

He snorted. "Wish I'd seen her. All we get around here are old people, usually." He squinted. "Wait. I do remember her. She was wearing a scarf around her neck, right?"

"Right! That's her. Do you know her? Her name's Leonie Winkler. I'm trying to find her."

He shook his head. "Never saw her before that. Sorry. I don't think she was a regular. But I only started here a few months ago."

Her thoughts whirled frantically. "Oh. Do you remember anything else about her? Did she tell you anything at all that might help me locate her?"

He stared at Diana. Then he looked down. "Oh, *ja.* I have her last-known address, blood-type, and DNA sample right here." When Diana frowned at him, he said, "I didn't even talk to her. How am I supposed to know anything? I just remember the scarf."

Letting out a breath of air, Diana walked, dejected, out the door, checking her phone. Moser hadn't called her back. And now, poor Dieter was probably locked up in prison. She'd put him there. An innocent kid who'd had nothing but hard knocks, his whole life.

She tilted her head to the sky and let out a groan of anguish.

When she looked down, though, she saw someone, standing behind a fenced tree on the sidewalk. Wearing sunglasses. Staring straight at her.

It was Marius Ugbodu.

She waved at him. Maybe he could help.

He turned and started to walk at a brisk pace, away from her.

"Wait! Wait, Agent Ugbodu!" she called, trying to catch up with him. She reached out and put a hand on his shoulder.

He stopped, and stiffly turned around. "I'm not an agent. Interpol doesn't have agents. I simply work with them. 'Mr. Ugbodu' or 'Marius' is fine."

"Okay, Marius," she said carefully. "You're clearly following me. Did Detective Moser tell you that they had arrested Dieter Hausman for the murder?"

He nodded.

"And yet, you're still—"

"Just because an arrest has been made, does not mean I can give up and go home. Besides, I saw Mr. Hausman. He doesn't seem quite bright enough, to me, to have killed Huber."

"I know, right?" Diana said, throwing up her hands. "I think that, too. I actually think I know who the real killer is, this time."

"You do, do you," he said, his eyes filled with doubt, and a bit of amusement she didn't quite understand. "Moser said you were the one who—"

"I know. I was wrong. But the thing is, I don't know how to find the person. She's the person who sold me the ticket. She used the name Leonie Winkler, but I don't know if that's her real name or not," she babbled.

"Leonie?" he said, reaching into the breast pocket of his dark suit. He produced a rumpled piece of paper, which he quickly unfolded. "Leonie Winkler. She's here."

Diana grabbed for the paper, but he held it firmly in his hands, she came around to look at it and realized it was a seating chart, for that night. There was Nina Horvath's name, just in the seat near the front row. Underneath, it said, *Floridusgasse* 56. Her address. Diana quickly scanned the seat she'd occupied. Sure enough, the name there was Leonie Winkler, *Lorbeergasse 12.*

Lorbeergasse 12. Lorbeergasse 12. Lorbeergasse 12. She repeated it in her head, over and over again, as he snatched the seating chart away from her.

"Well, that's it. That's what I need. You see, I think that maybe she was in love with Huber, one of his women, and he broke it off with her, so she---"

"You know what I think?" he said, his coal black eyes, intent on her.

"No . . ." At that moment, she really didn't care. All she cared about was getting a cab and taking it to *Lorbeergasse 12.* They had to move quickly. For Dieter's sake.

"I think you know that they're going to find out that Dieter's innocent, so you're lining up your next victim to take the fall."

Diana froze. "What?"

"These murders . . . it's no coincidence, is it?" He said, eyeing her, stroking his chin astutely. "You've known, right along, just what you're doing. You thrill in creating these murders that you can blame on an innocent person. Admit it. Admit that you're the killer."

Her jaw dropped. She stood there, frozen, unable to get her mouth to form words. Finally, she was able to collect herself enough to respond.

"Are you insane?" She took a step away. "I won't admit that! It's not true."

"I think I should have Detective Moser take you in for questioning. I guarantee all these murders will suddenly stop."

She could tell from the way he was standing there, his hand in his pocket, that he was ready to move. Arrest her, throw her in jail, do everything possible to convince the rest of them that she was the guilty one. Her eyes shifted from side to side. He began to advance.

The second he did, she said, "There he is! Johann Strauss!" and pointed behind him.

He whirled.

She took off in a mad dash, running around the corner and into a marketplace filled with people, lugging her bag with her. Skirting around people in her way, she ran herself breathless, still unsure of where she was heading. When she felt like she could run no more, she threw herself flush against a wall and watched, in disbelief, as Ugbodu rushed right past her.

Letting out a sigh, she quickly retraced her steps to the main road and held up her hand to hail a cab.

Lorbeergasse 12. There was no time to waste.

*

The cab let Diana off on a small side-street in the middle of the city, in front of a stately, white brick home with black shutters that looked both elegant and historic. Leonie Winkler, if that was her name, had exuded sophistication, wealth and elegance, and this home fit her to a tee.

Diana looked up and down the street, expecting to see a cab holding Ugbodu, heading toward her. But despite being central to everything, the street itself was quiet enclave, with mostly residential homes and little traffic.

Diana took a deep breath and looked up at the home. She recalled being a bit envious of Leonie Winkler—she'd had beauty, wealth, and a young family, not to mention the means to visit *Musikverein* whenever she wanted. What could have driven the woman inside this house to murder? Was it even possible? Diana stood there, shuddering, hardly able to believe it.

Ugbodu will be here any moment. You'd better go in and find out if your big idea is correct, soon, before he comes and arrests you.

She climbed the steps and knocked on the door, her hand shaking. She was still determining what to say when she heard movement inside. Eventually, she settled on a story—she'd just happened by to thank Leonie for the ticket. That was believable.

A moment later, the same dark-haired beauty who'd sat across from her in café Johann Strauss answered. She was wearing a pale pink blouse and slacks, her face and hair as made up as before, as if she was about to go out. Or maybe that was how she dressed all the time? Diana couldn't imagine a moment when this woman wasn't looking absolutely picture-perfect.

And she was wearing the pendant, resting in the hollow of her throat. The gray-and-amber striped disc. From here, she could even see the great red spot on its surface. Huber hadn't named that symphony for the god. He'd named it after the planet.

Leonie clearly didn't recognize her, because she frowned and tilted her head. "*Ja?*"

"Leonie Winkler?" Diana blurted.

"*Ja?*" She seemed even more confused. So that really was her name.

Diana patted her chest. "It's me. Diana St. James. You sold me the ticket for the concert a couple days ago at *Musikverein*?"

"Oh, right." Her pretty features seemed to wrinkle in confusion. "How did you know where to find me?"

A car went by on the street behind Diana. She looked over her shoulder. Not Ogbodu, thankfully. She said, "I asked around! I was so happy to be at the concert—it really was a once in a lifetime opportunity, that I felt like I simply must thank you before I left Vienna. So, thank you."

"You . . . asked around?"

Diana nodded. "The box office told me that the seat had been registered to you."

"Oh, it shouldn't have been registered to me. It was one of—" She stopped and pulled at the collar of her blouse. "I mean, that's nice. I'm glad you had a great time. No need to thank me. It's a lovely theater."

She started to close the door, but Diana blurted, "I feel terrible that you missed such an amazing performance. I mean, the orchestra was wonderful. But that pianist! Oh, he was simply divine. I feel like I need to find out when his next performance is, so I can kill, steal, or beg to get a ticket for it."

The woman stared at Diana, her face a mix of astonishment and disgust. "Oh, dear. Did you not hear the news? It's been all over Vienna."

"What news?" Diana said, feigning innocence.

"Lukas Huber is dead. They say it happened right after the performance, that night."

"*Dead?*" Diana allowed her jaw to hang open for a beat. "You can't be serious."

"Unfortunately, I am," she said, absently fingering her necklace.

"I can't believe it! Did he have a heart condition? All that pounding the keys, I can imagine, would take a lot out of a person."

"No, he was murdered. In his dressing room," she said rather tonelessly, as if such a thing happened all the time.

Diana clapped a hand over her mouth. "Goodness! That's awful. How horrible. Do they know who did it?"

"I don't—I don't know," she said, her eyes shifted awkwardly away as she started to close the door some more. "I'm sorry to be the bearer of such bad news. He was a talent."

There's something she's hiding, Diana thought immediately. *I need to find out what it is.*

Behind her, a car turned onto the street. Diana couldn't be sure, but it looked like a taxi. She felt jittery and anxious. Waving her hand in front of her face, she began to hyperventilate. "This is terrible. Oh, I feel faint."

The woman stared at her in horror. "Are you okay?"

"Could I trouble you for a glass of water?" she said, fanning herself more furiously.

"Well . . ." The woman opened the door a bit more, allowing Diana to brazenly move her way through. Leonie shrugged. "Yes. Of course. Please. Come in."

Good, Diana thought, stepping through the threshold. *Now maybe I can see who Leonie Winkler really is.*

CHAPTER TWENTY SIX

Diana followed Leonie through a narrow foyer, and through double doors. "Have a seat," her host said woodenly. "I'll just be a moment."

Diana found herself in a sun-filled room with black and white striped wallpaper. While something like that would've normally made Diana think of a prison, Leonie had pulled it off. The room was homey and yet chic, with modern, comfortable blue denim sofas and a large brick fireplace. Diana sat on the edge of one of the ladder-backed accent chairs as Leonie went to fetch the water. Her eyes volleyed around the room as she heard the water running at the kitchen sink.

They landed on a massive black-and-white picture, over the mantle. Diana had seen it before, carried by the many fans outside Lukas Huber's dressing room, and during the vigil. It was the picture of Lukas Huber, looking as pompous as ever, arms crossed, sitting beside his grand piano. From his Sony recording, *Lukas Huber! Live and Personal in Paris!*

She stood up and went toward it but stopped when something else caught her eye. There was a Bose sound system on one of the built-in bookshelves, and next to it, rows and rows of CDs. Diana went closer, expecting to see a wealth of different music from various performers.

Instead, she saw only one.

There was, obviously, a well-worn and loved copy of *Lukas Huber! Live and Personal in Paris!* But also, *Lukas Huber in Berlin—Recorded Live! Lukas Huber plays Chopin's Greatest Works. Lukas Huber and the Chicago Symphony Orchestra play Mendelssohn. The St. Petersburg Philharmonic and Lukas Huber—an Evening of Rachmaninoff*. . .

And on and on. In fact, there wasn't a single CD that wasn't Lukas Huber. Not one at all.

Diana was so fascinated by it that she didn't hear Leonie coming up behind her under a floorboard shifted in the entrance. When she whirled, Leonie was staring at her, a cautious look on her face. "Your water?" She held the glass out.

"Thank you. Perfect." Diana took it and sucked in a large gulp. "Whew. I feel better now. I see you were a big fan."

She nodded stiffly. "Oh, yes. That was why I was very sad I couldn't go," she said, taking the glass back from Diana. "Now, if you'll excuse me—"

"Why weren't you able to be there again?" Diana asked quickly, as something came to her. "Didn't you—"

"I just wasn't—"

"You'd said something about not being able to get a sitter for your child, right?"

The woman swallowed. "Yes. That's right."

Diana nodded. "Ah." But as Diana looked around, she saw no toys. No discarded blankies. No sippy cups. No baby photos, anywhere. In fact, the only prominent photo in the room was that of Lukas Huber. Other than that, the place was like a museum, where children would be expressly prohibited.

Leonie seemed to realize it at the same moment, because she laughed lightly and said, "We're divorced. The child's husband and me. The child is with him for an outing, so I have the afternoon to myself."

The child. It sounded so cold and impersonal. Phony. Diana said, "Boy or girl? I don't think you told me."

"Girl," she said quickly.

"Right, I think you did tell me that. How old?" Diana blurted, getting more excited now.

"Just under a year."

"Oh, lovely. What a wonderful age. Walking yet?" Her words were coming a mile a minute now, as if she was an attorney questioning a suspect, on the brink of getting a confession.

Diana could sense that Leonie was getting defensive from the way she crossed her arms and stammered, "Uh . . .no."

Calm it down a little, Diana. She smiled widely. "It's so cute when they're crawling all over the place. What's her name?"

Leonie's frown deepened. "What—why are you asking all these personal questions? I appreciate you coming by to thank me for the ticket, but like I said, it's not necessary. I think it's time that you left, now."

"All right, all right," Diana said brightly, trying not to rouse suspicions. But the woman was clearly suspicious. And she still hadn't gotten what she came for. She followed Leonie out to the hallway, her mind cycling through possible stalling techniques. Should she pretend to choke, now? No, she'd already used the "health emergency" ruse. She needed to think, quick.

Her mind was still blank when Leonie put a hand on the front doorknob.

Suddenly, she blurted, "That's quite a collection. You must really love classical music!"

She nodded. "Indeed."

"I mean, for you to go to *Musikverein* by yourself. When I was married, I never would've thought of doing such a thing without my husband. Even after we were divorced, it was really hard for me to go places, alone."

Leonie turned. "How did . . ." She paused, as something seemed to cross her mind. "Well . . . we weren't married very long, so--"

"Tickets to the music hall are hard to come by. Many of them are legacy tickets, passed down from generation to generation. Or they're available as a subscription, to the entire season. And single tickets are often taken by the performers themselves, for guests. I learned that from the box office at *Theater an de Wien*. So you and your husband didn't go to the symphony together?"

She shook her head. "No. My husband was not interested in classical music, so—"

"That necklace is really nice. It's Jupiter, isn't it?"

Leonie's hand flew to her chest. "Well, yes, but—"

"Like the Jupiter Symphony. Did Lukas Huber give that to you?"

She swallowed. "What?"

"There is no husband, is there? The necklace, and the ticket were given to you by Lukas Huber, weren't they? The seat was one of the many seats he secured to give to the women he wooed."

The woman's eyes widened, and she took a step back, as if trapped. "What are you saying?"

"I'm saying that you killed Lukas Huber. You sold the ticket to me so that it wouldn't appear that your name was anywhere near the music hall when it happened. Then you sneaked in the back, avoiding the lax security, and waited in his dressing room. You were there when he entered, and you killed him. But you didn't know that Lukas Huber had added your name to the guest list. You thought it was just anonymous. Right?"

Leonie's face was red. *That's not the face of an innocent woman.* "You're crazy. I think you should go now," she said, her voice barely a whisper, as she reached for the door.

She pulled it open a bit, but Diana reached over and closed it. "I'm not going anywhere until you admit what you did," she said, her voice a low whisper.

Leonie Winkler looked at Diana, then at the door, then at Diana again, and her face twisted into a scowl. The transformation from elegant debutante to devil was instantaneous, and quite remarkable. When she spoke next, her once-soft, musical voice was now cold and low. "I don't think you want to do that, Ms. St. James."

Diana shuddered as her eyes darted toward the door, and from side to side, looking for a way to leave. But the way was blocked. At that moment, she had to agree with Leonie. Because now she was here, alone, in the house of a murderer, and there was no escape.

CHAPTER TWENTY SEVEN

Leonie Winkler pressed her slim body against the door and dragged in a breath. She let it out slowly, and the next time she spoke, she was more her regular self. "You don't understand. This isn't my fault." She patted her chest with both hands. "I'm the victim here. Really. You wouldn't believe what he put me through."

Diana's throat had gone dry, but she managed to squeak out, "Did Lukas Huber give you the ticket to his performance?"

She nodded. "Of course. He's given me *many* tickets to his performances, over the past few months. So I thought--" She stopped abruptly and shook her head.

"You thought you were the only one."

She looked at the ground. Her voice was small. "Yes. It turns out that he had many women. At first, I thought you might be one of them, too. He loved women. Too much. Probably even more than the music."

"Were you engaged to him?"

"Almost. He wined and dined me, whenever we were both in town. I'm an interior designer so I travel a lot, and so did he. But whenever we found ourselves in Vienna at the same time, we always would get together. And it was love. I was absolutely, head over heels, in love with Lukas. Sure, I knew he had millions of female fans, but I thought I was the special one. I thought it was a perfect relationship, and that he'd soon propose to me. He'd hinted at it," she said hopefully, but suddenly, her tone changed, becoming bitter and sarcastic. "And then I found out he was simply playing me. I found out that he had half a dozen seats in every hall, in every country, that he kept filled, giving them to a rotating assortment of *other* women. Paid escorts, prostitutes, beautiful women of all walks of life, he'd meet and collect . . . he didn't discriminate. He had them, all over the world, and I was just one of many women he liked to string along."

Diana's heart hurt for the girl. She knew betrayal, too. Though Evan had the decency to ask Diana for a divorce prior to dating Tilda, his now-fiancé, it still hurt to know the man you loved had moved on to other women. "I'm sorry. How did you find out?"

She snorted. “It was stupid, really. He was so careful, so good at hiding it, all the dozens of women he had all over. I never suspected anything. For months and months, I thought I was the only one. And then he sent me one text from New York, and it was suspicious. It had nothing to do with what we were talking about, but it was odd and flirtatious. And that one text brought everything down. I didn’t question him. The next time I met with him, I figured out the password to his phone, and I checked it. And I found all these names. All these women. He’d been stringing me along forever.” Hands on hips, she paced in front of the door. “I can’t even explain to you how betrayed I felt. This was the man I loved. The man I had given everything in my life to. And I was nothing to him. Just a game. He wanted to see how long he could string me along for.”

Leonie swung around and met Diana’s eyes, as if prompting her to say that it was all right, that she understood.

“That’s awful,” Diana offered. She could imagine how terrible something like that would feel, but she couldn’t say she understood. How could anyone be so hurt that they would consider murder as an acceptable response?

“I didn’t tell him that I knew. He played the message off like he was tired after his concert, and that was all, but every time we were together after that, I thought about it. I was just biding time, waiting. I’d been in his dressing room before. I knew how lax security was back there, and that there were no cameras. I knew just how to get in there without being seen, and how to escape afterwards. Selling the ticket to you was the easy part. He didn’t even notice I wasn’t there. I always thought he didn’t look at me because he thought I’d make him nervous. I didn’t realize there were dozens of other women who were also thinking the same thing.”

“When did you go backstage?”

It was after the Unfinished Symphony. I went in the back. I heard the last notes of it and saw him getting ready to walk out on stage. He never even saw me—he gets so wrapped up in his music and his own ego that he doesn’t notice anything. It was simple. He walked out, and I walked into his dressing room.” She smiled. “I waited there, listening to the whole thing. You know, the Jupiter Symphony, he said he’d written for me. That I was his muse.”

Her face fell and turned downright frightening, twisting in anger.

"And it was that music that played in my head when he came back, I crept up on him, and strangled him with his own cravat. He saw me in the vanity mirror . . . I know he did. And I'd like to think that maybe, for the first time in his life, he actually regretted something he'd done." She shrugged. "I'm not the least bit sorry. The man was a pig. He gave me gifts, told me I was everything to him. And every last word out of his mouth was a filthy lie, made to bolster his own ego. He had a lone line of groupies that he was just rotating around, from town to town. He deserved to die, and I'm sure I'm not the only person to think so. If I hadn't done it, one of them, I'm sure, would have."

"But you did it," Diana whispered, still looking at the door. "You killed him."

"Yes. I did. And like I said, I'd do it again. In a heartbeat." She smiled and glanced into the living room, at the photograph of him, above her mantle. "The funny thing is that he always believed he was a rock star, kind of like Liszt. He thought he would be memorialized for hundreds of years in the future, and that Vienna would erect a statue to him in a park somewhere. But he was wrong. That'll never happen. Not now. He'll never be considered one of the greats. In fact, there's talk that he actually stole some of the lesser-known works of other artists. And I don't doubt it one bit. He was snake."

"Well," Diana said, as lightly as she could. "On that note . . ."

She pointed to the door.

Leonie planted her feet in front of it, an incredulous expression on her face. "You didn't think I was going to let you leave, did you?"

"Well . . ." *I was hoping you would, truthfully.*

Diana's mouth went dry as the pretty woman reached into the pocket of her pants and pulled out a long cord. Her eyes were wild, unfocused. Insane. She breathed, "I did it once before. I can do it again," and wrapped the cord around each hand, pulling it taut in front of her.

Diana had no doubt that she would. She held up her hands, her heartbeat pounding in her ears. "Now, don't get crazy. Of course, I won't tell a soul. I just wanted to come here and thank you. That's all. Now that I've done that, I'll just be on my way to the train stat—"

"Don't be ridiculous. I'm not letting you walk out."

Diana inhaled sharply. "The police will be here. I already called them."

Leonie laughed bitterly. "Right. Then where are they? You're bluffing."

"I'm –"

Before she could say more, the woman's face went rigid into a mask of hate and determination as she lunged forward. Diana let out a cry and backed away, then rushed the first place she could find—up the staircase to the second floor, her feet scuffing on the hardwood.

Leonie was right behind her, heels clicking noisily on the hard surface. "Stop!" she shouted. "Don't you go away from me. Come back here!"

Diana reached the top of the landing and flew into the nearest room, a neat bedroom with nothing more than a carefully made bed with a flowered duvet cover. She tried to close the door, but when she'd slammed it, found that there was no lock. She scanned the room, looking for an open window. *Smart move, Diana. Now you're on the second floor. Good luck climbing out.* Instead, she found a closed one. She rushed to it, trying to pull it open, so that at least she could shout for help, but though she managed to unlock it, it was stuck. She pulled and tried to budge it with the heel of her hand, but it went nowhere.

By then, Leonie was standing in the doorway. Trapped, Diana looked over her shoulder.

Leonie was smiling a sick, sadistic smile. She knew she had pinned her quarry as she lifted the cord to wrap it around Diana's neck. Diana's hand instinctively flew to her throat as she imagined the tug of the cord around it, the gasping for air. "Listen to me. Be reasonable. If you kill another person, this will only be worse for you."

Leonie shrugged, laughing. "Not if no one ever finds out. And who are you? A tourist? No one even knows or cares about you around here. No one will even notice you're missing."

Diana stared. Even most murderers took no joy from committing murder. But Leonie Winkler was actually laughing at the prospect of taking someone's life.

This woman wasn't just a jilted lover. No, she was stark, raving mad.

And that meant . . . *There's no way you're going to talk sense into her. Your only hope is to escape.*

Diana's eyes darted to the side, looking for escape as the small woman advanced. In the very moment that Leonie lunged forward, letting out an animal cry, Diana noticed the other door and made a break for it, sliding across the wall and pulling it open.

She expected a closet, something she could possibly hide in while she called the authorities. Instead, she found another room. But not just a room, she realized, as she whirled around and saw dozens—hundreds, maybe—of sets of eyes, staring back at her. All of them belonged to the same, smug, egotistical man she'd seen on the stage at *Musikverien*, just days ago.

Lukas Huber.

He was there in blown-up, life-size cardboard cutouts. Framed programs. Record covers. Piles and piles of CDs and DVDs. Posters. And absolutely every inch of the room was covered in photographs of the late virtuoso, staring down upon her. No, this wasn't a room. It was a shrine.

Diana could only stare in shock. It gave Leonie the time she needed to come up behind Diana and slip the cord over her head. Before it could find its place, snug around her neck, Diana's hands flew to it, fingers locking around it, she pulled on it for all she was worth, loosening it, and managed to scramble out of its chokehold.

Backing away, she grabbed hold of the first thing she could find—a CD entitled *Live from Tokyo!* and chucked it at Leonie.

Leonie let out a cry, but undaunted, kept coming.

Diana reached over and grabbed another, and another, throwing as much as she could get her hands on. DVDs, CDs, even a little bobble-head sculpture of the man. She tossed everything she could find. The pointed corner of a CD smacked into Leonie's cheek, leaving an instant red welt. She shrieked. "Don't you touch my things, you witch!" she shouted, holding her hands up for protection.

Eventually, Diana was out of things to throw. Leonie, cheek now bleeding, long dark hair a wild mess, had transformed into some kind of rabid animal, intent on capturing Diana. Helpless, she scuttled behind the life-sized cardboard cutout of Lukas Huber, at his piano, and nearly tripped over something. She reached down to pick it up and realized it was a framed photograph. She lifted it and stared at the picture of Leonie Winkler and Lukas Huber, gazing at one another and smiling, and looking very much in love.

So it wasn't just in her head, Diana thought. *He really did string her along.*

Leonie's eyes widened as she saw the photograph. She let out a sad moan. "Please. Put that down. That's the only photograph I have of me—and him—together."

Diana held the picture more tightly. Finally, she had some leverage, something to use against her. She motioned like she was going to throw it. Leonie flinched.

"Drop the cord," Diana said, her voice unwavering.

For a moment, it looked as though she had Leonie right where she wanted her. She started to lower her hands, and her shoulders slumped slightly.

But then, with a loud, rabid cry, she rushed forward, teeth bared in attack, hands ready to strike.

Diana lifted the frame into the air, and with a swift, clean motion, brought it down, hard, right on Leonie's head. Glass shattered, and Leonie let out a grunt before collapsing to the ground in a heap.

Diana stared at the motionless figure at her feet, heart beating like mad.

There was a sound in the hallway, shifting floorboards. Still gripping the ruined frame in her hands, Diana looked up, just as Marius Ugbodu and Detective Moser came through the doors.

Her body sagged against the wall in relief. "This is Leonie Winkler. The person who killed Lukas Huber," Diana said breathlessly.

"Now, where have I heard that before?" Detective Moser said, as he looked around. "What the . . ."

"She was obsessed. A jilted lover," Diana explained.

Ugbodu said, "You say that. But where's your proof?"

"She told me! She confessed. She tried to kill me, too," Diana explained. "She told me that she thought they were going to get engaged, but then she learned he had a lot of other women. And since she'd been to many of his concerts, she knew that the security would be lax. She knew how to avoid it all. She was waiting in his dressing room when he got there."

"She confessed to *you*, maybe," Ugbodu said.

Moser nudged him. "Look around you. This woman clearly has something wrong with her."

Detective Moser cleared away the glass and turned Leonie over. She was semi-conscious, trying to blink her eyes open. He snapped some cuffs on the woman and said, "You're coming with us, down to the station."

She seemed to awaken with the sound of the cuffs being placed on her and looked around. Scowling at Diana, she snapped, "I knew you'd tell someone! And fine. I don't care. I'm glad you know. I'm glad everyone knows! I'm happy he's dead."

"Aha!" Diana shouted. "I told you!"

Moser froze, then brought her to her feet and looked at her. For the first time, Diana was sure she could see a smile on his face. "Thanks for the confession. You are going to jail for a very long time." He led her out the door.

Ugbodu lingered, watching Diana as she clasped at her chest, willing her breathing to return to normal. "So I suppose you're innocent. Again."

She smiled. "I told you I was."

"Yes," he said, refusing to return that smile. Did he smile? Was he even capable of such a thing? She wasn't sure about that. "And I'm assuming that you'll be moving on again?"

"That's right."

"And where will you be off to?"

She shrugged. "I don't know. I'm thinking Barcelona, maybe. I was on my way there when this idea about Leonie Winkler suddenly occurred to me. She was the one who sold me the ticket. She told me she couldn't make it because she couldn't find a sitter. When I realized that it was just a single ticket, I remembered what I'd been told at the box office."

"Which was?"

"That the best single tickets were usually reserved for the performers themselves. Meaning that Lukas Huber had personally given her a ticket. And that was when I knew her story was a lie, and she was more than just a fan—she knew him personally."

He nodded, and for a split second, she almost allowed herself to believe that he looked a bit impressed with her. But then he shrugged. "You'd better go catch your train."

"Thank you." She began to step over the piles of tossed CD and other Lukas Huber memorabilia, on her way to the stairs.

"And Ms. St. James?"

She whirled. "Yes?"

His voice was more of a threat than a goodbye. "Stay out of trouble."

She nodded. She had no doubt, that if she didn't, she would see him again.

But for now? A new country, and new possibilities, awaited. And she couldn't wait.

EPILOGUE

As Diana stood at the platform, waiting for the next train to Barcelona, she got a text from Detective Moser. *Dieter's being released as we speak. He isn't too angry at you.*

After the excitement with Leonie Winkler, she'd decided to have dinner in Vienna and take the late-night train out, so that she could sleep for most of the twenty-hour excursion through Zurich. She'd thought a lot, though, about poor Dieter, and the strife she must've put the young man through. So this was very welcome news.

Please, tell him I'm sorry again, she typed in.

A moment later, he responded with, *He says no hard feelings. He also says he should be thanking you because you inspired him to audition for the principal pianist position at the Philharmonic. He says that if you come back to Musikverein, he'll save you a seat.*

She smiled. Right now, she couldn't see herself coming back anytime soon. But she could definitely see the name *Dieter Hausman* in lights, all over the world, just as the name *Lukas Huber* had been. And maybe he'd actually compose his very own stuff, without having to steal from the greats.

Maybe, then, she'd come back to Vienna and finally be moved to tears.

But for now, it was time to move on, and she was excited to shake off the dust of this city and head onto the next leg of her journey.

She peered down the rails and saw the headlight of the bullet train, nearing. She looked around, taking in that one last look of Vienna, and breathed deeply, savoring her last taste of Vienna air. Then, as she lifted the bag at her feet, she heard it.

Her last bit of Vienna music. She recognized it instantly. It was Aase's Death, from Peer Gynt, by Edvard Grieg, but where she was used to hearing the recording in her grandmother's house performed by an entire orchestra, the sound was coming from a lone violin. It was fragile, and heart-wrenching.

She looked up to see a little boy, no more than seven or eight, dressed in jeans and a t-shirt, standing near a pillar, his violin case open in front of him. He was busking for change, but at that moment, money seemed to be the last thing on his mind. He was moving the bow so effortlessly across the strings, his eyes closed, as if he was the only person in the world and completely in tune with the music.

Diana heaved in an uneven breath as she listened, letting the mournful song set her spirits aloft. She thought of the many problems she'd had on this trip, with her family, the murders, the missed connections and skipped sightseeing opportunities, all the other obstacles that had settled in her way and seemed so insurmountable, and her heart felt light. This wasn't a race, or a competition, or an escape, and it certainly wasn't about ticking off points on a map. Everything seemed so trivial now. What mattered was that she was here, and the world was open for her, waiting for her to discover, and discover herself. That was all there was to it, to this crazy journey. Discovering herself.

She only knew she was crying when she felt the lone tear, making its way down her cheek, past her lips, and dangling off the end of her chin.

When the train pulled into the station, she walked over to the little boy, who'd just finished playing his tune, and dropped a few euros into his case. He nodded, his blonde curls bouncing, and said, "*Danke sehr aufmerksam.*"

She wasn't quite sure what that meant, but she knew enough to understand that Danke meant "thank you," so she shook her head. "No. *Danke* to you. You have no idea what your playing meant for me."

The little boy grinning, showing two missing front teeth. *"Auf Wiedersehen!"*

"Goodbye!" she said, hoisting her bag onto her shoulder and climbing onto the train.

She couldn't stop smiling as she settled herself into her seat and got herself comfortable for the long journey ahead. She pulled out her journal and happily marked a line through the words, *Be moved to tears by beautiful music.*

Her phone buzzed with a text from Bea: *Hai took me out for sushi. It's actually not that terrible. In fact, I'm craving a dragon roll right now.*

She laughed. That was Bea, rushing head-first into battle without knowing who her opponent was. She typed in: *I knew it would work out. Love you. On to Barcelona.*

Bea responded with: *Love you, too, Mommy. Have a great time.* ☺

Picking up her journal, she turned the page and wrote: *Barcelona.*

Now, she thought, *what do I want to do there?*

As she was trying to decide, her phone started to ring with an unfamiliar number. For a moment, she thought about not answering, but in the last second, she decided to pick up. "Hello?"

"Is this the lovely Diana St. James?"

She recognized the accent at once, and her pulse thrummed with excitement. It was her old Irish friend that she'd met in Paris, Sean. It felt like ages since she'd last seen him, when he'd been ready to travel off somewhere . . . He, too, said he'd be tooling around Europe for the next few months, and hoped that maybe they'd run into one another. "Sean? How nice to hear from you!"

"That's me, love. How are you making your way through Europe?"

"Very well, thanks. I'm in Vienna, now, but just getting on a train. Heading out tonight."

"Where are you heading to?"

"Barcelona, by way of Zurich. Where are you?"

"Barcelona, eh? You were talking about going there the last time we saw each other, I think. What happened?"

"Oh. I flipped that coin like you told me to, and it landed on heads, so I went to Florence instead!"

"Ah. Well, now I think it's time you explore the tail-end of that coin. And I think that's a sign. I haven't made my way up to Ballygangargin just yet. I'm here in Portugal. What do you say I meet you halfway?"

"Halfway?" Her heart started to beat madly. "You really would?"

"That's right, lass, I was thinking that should be my next stop, anyway. And I'd love to see you."

"Great! I'll be there tomorrow evening." She checked her ticket. "At eight. You'll meet me at the station?"

"It's a date. I look forward to seeing you, love. Say hello to Austria for me." He ended the call, and she found herself grinning some more as she stared out the window. Without her realizing it, the train had begun pulling from the station, and now Vienna was disappearing from view as the skies darkened.

She reached into her bag and found the coin Sean had given her in Paris, to flip so she could make her decision between Florence and Barcelona. It was old, and more octagonal than circular, with what looked like Gaelic runes upon it. She wasn't sure if she believed that certain items could bring good luck, but she held it close to her heart and stroked its raised surface, she felt for sure it was possible to will things into existence, if only a person dreamed about them enough.

After all, she'd finally been moved to tears by music, which proved that she wasn't as jaded as she thought. So maybe that meant that she wasn't too old to find love?

She stared down at the empty page, then uncapped her pen and began to write.

NOW AVAILABLE FOR PRE-ORDER!

A FATALITY IN SPAIN

(A Year in Europe—Book 4)

"When you think that life cannot get better, Blake Pierce comes up with another masterpiece of thriller and mystery! This book is full of twists, and the end brings a surprising revelation. Strongly recommended for the permanent library of any reader who enjoys a very well-written thriller."

--Books and Movie Reviews (re *Almost Gone*)

A FATALITY IN SPAIN is book #4 in a charming new cozy mystery series by USA Today bestselling author Blake Pierce, whose #1 bestseller *Once Gone* has received 1,500 five-star reviews. The series (A YEAR IN EUROPE) begins with book #1 (A MURDER IN PARIS).

Diana Hope, 55, is still adjusting to her recent separation when she discovers her ex-husband has just proposed to a woman 30 years younger. Secretly hoping they would reunite, Diana is devastated. She realizes the time has come to reimagine life without him—in fact, to reimagine her life, period.

Devoting the last 30 years of her life to being a dutiful wife and mother and to climbing the corporate ladder, Diana has been relentlessly driven, and has not taken a moment to do anything for herself. Now, the time has come.

Diana never forgot her first boyfriend, who begged her to join him for a year in Europe after college. She had wanted to go so badly, but it had seemed like a wild, romantic idea, and a gap year, she'd thought, would hinder her resume and career. But now, with her daughters grown, her husband gone, and her career no longer fulfilling, Diana realizes it's time for herself—and to take that romantic year in Europe she'd always dreamed of.

Diana prepares to embark on the year of her life, finally turning to her bucket list, hoping to tour the most beautiful sights and sample the most scrumptious cuisines—and maybe, even, to fall in love again. But a year in Europe may have different plans in store for her. Can A-type Diana learn to go with the flow, to be spontaneous, to let down her guard and to learn to truly enjoy life again?

In A FATALITY IN SPAIN (Book #4), Diana decides to let go and take a chance at love, meeting up with her newfound friend in Barcelona, and trying to muster the courage to fulfill her lifelong dream of running with the bulls in Pamplona. Between the great food, the sunny streets, and her new love, life seems alive again—until a murder turns her world upside down. Can Diana save the case and herself—along with her summer?

A YEAR IN EUROPE is a charming and laugh-out-loud cozy mystery series, packed with food and travel, with mysteries that will leave you on the edge of your seat, and with experiences that will leave you with a sense of wonder. As Diana embarks on her quixotic quest for love and meaning, you will find yourself falling in love and rooting for her. You will be in shock at the twists and turns her journey takes as she somehow finds herself at the center of a mystery, and must play amateur sleuth to solve it. Fans of books like *Eat, Pray, Love* and *Under the Tuscan Sun* have finally found the cozy mystery series they've been hoping for!

SCANDAL IN LONDON (Book #5), AN IMPOSTER IN DUBLIN (Book #6), SEDUCTION IN BORDEAUX (Book #7), JEALOUSY IN SWITZERLAND (Book #8), and A DEBACLE IN PRAGUE (Book #9) are now also available!

Blake Pierce

Blake Pierce is the USA Today bestselling author of the RILEY PAGE mystery series, which includes seventeen books. Blake Pierce is also the author of the MACKENZIE WHITE mystery series, comprising fourteen books; of the AVERY BLACK mystery series, comprising six books; of the KERI LOCKE mystery series, comprising five books; of the MAKING OF RILEY PAIGE mystery series, comprising six books; of the KATE WISE mystery series, comprising seven books; of the CHLOE FINE psychological suspense mystery, comprising six books; of the JESSIE HUNT psychological suspense thriller series, comprising nineteen books, of the AU PAIR psychological suspense thriller series, comprising three books; of the ZOE PRIME mystery series, comprising six books; of the ADELE SHARP mystery series, comprising thirteen books; of the EUROPEAN VOYAGE cozy mystery series, comprising six books; of the new LAURA FROST FBI suspense thriller, comprising four books (and counting); of the new ELLA DARK FBI suspense thriller, comprising six books (and counting); of the A YEAR IN EUROPE cozy mystery series, comprising nine books (and counting); of the AVA GOLD mystery series, comprising three books (and counting); and of the RACHEL GIFT mystery series, comprising three books (and counting).

An avid reader and lifelong fan of the mystery and thriller genres, Blake loves to hear from you, so please feel free to visit www.blakepierceauthor.com to learn more and stay in touch.

BOOKS BY BLAKE PIERCE

RACHEL GIFT MYSTERY SERIES
HER LAST WISH (Book #1)
HER LAST CHANCE (Book #2)
HER LAST HOPE (Book #3)

AVA GOLD MYSTERY SERIES
CITY OF PREY (Book #1)
CITY OF FEAR (Book #2)
CITY OF BONES (Book #3)

A YEAR IN EUROPE
A MURDER IN PARIS (Book #1)
DEATH IN FLORENCE (Book #2)
VENGEANCE IN VIENNA (Book #3)
A FATALITY IN SPAIN (Book #4)
SCANDAL IN LONDON (Book #5)
AN IMPOSTOR IN DUBLIN (Book #6)
SEDUCTION IN BORDEAUX (Book #7)
JEALOUSY IN SWITZERLAND (Book #8)
A DEBACLE IN PRAGUE (Book #9)

ELLA DARK FBI SUSPENSE THRILLER
GIRL, ALONE (Book #1)
GIRL, TAKEN (Book #2)
GIRL, HUNTED (Book #3)
GIRL, SILENCED (Book #4)
GIRL, VANISHED (Book 5)
GIRL ERASED (Book #6)

LAURA FROST FBI SUSPENSE THRILLER
ALREADY GONE (Book #1)
ALREADY SEEN (Book #2)
ALREADY TRAPPED (Book #3)
ALREADY MISSING (Book #4)

EUROPEAN VOYAGE COZY MYSTERY SERIES
MURDER (AND BAKLAVA) (Book #1)

DEATH (AND APPLE STRUDEL) (Book #2)
CRIME (AND LAGER) (Book #3)
MISFORTUNE (AND GOUDA) (Book #4)
CALAMITY (AND A DANISH) (Book #5)
MAYHEM (AND HERRING) (Book #6)

ADELE SHARP MYSTERY SERIES
LEFT TO DIE (Book #1)
LEFT TO RUN (Book #2)
LEFT TO HIDE (Book #3)
LEFT TO KILL (Book #4)
LEFT TO MURDER (Book #5)
LEFT TO ENVY (Book #6)
LEFT TO LAPSE (Book #7)
LEFT TO VANISH (Book #8)
LEFT TO HUNT (Book #9)
LEFT TO FEAR (Book #10)
LEFT TO PREY (Book #11)
LEFT TO LURE (Book #12)
LEFT TO CRAVE (Book #13)

THE AU PAIR SERIES
ALMOST GONE (Book#1)
ALMOST LOST (Book #2)
ALMOST DEAD (Book #3)

ZOE PRIME MYSTERY SERIES
FACE OF DEATH (Book#1)
FACE OF MURDER (Book #2)
FACE OF FEAR (Book #3)
FACE OF MADNESS (Book #4)
FACE OF FURY (Book #5)
FACE OF DARKNESS (Book #6)

A JESSIE HUNT PSYCHOLOGICAL SUSPENSE SERIES
THE PERFECT WIFE (Book #1)
THE PERFECT BLOCK (Book #2)
THE PERFECT HOUSE (Book #3)
THE PERFECT SMILE (Book #4)

THE PERFECT LIE (Book #5)
THE PERFECT LOOK (Book #6)
THE PERFECT AFFAIR (Book #7)
THE PERFECT ALIBI (Book #8)
THE PERFECT NEIGHBOR (Book #9)
THE PERFECT DISGUISE (Book #10)
THE PERFECT SECRET (Book #11)
THE PERFECT FAÇADE (Book #12)
THE PERFECT IMPRESSION (Book #13)
THE PERFECT DECEIT (Book #14)
THE PERFECT MISTRESS (Book #15)
THE PERFECT IMAGE (Book #16)
THE PERFECT VEIL (Book #17)
THE PERFECT INDISCRETION (Book #18)
THE PERFECT RUMOR (Book #19)

CHLOE FINE PSYCHOLOGICAL SUSPENSE SERIES
NEXT DOOR (Book #1)
A NEIGHBOR'S LIE (Book #2)
CUL DE SAC (Book #3)
SILENT NEIGHBOR (Book #4)
HOMECOMING (Book #5)
TINTED WINDOWS (Book #6)

KATE WISE MYSTERY SERIES
IF SHE KNEW (Book #1)
IF SHE SAW (Book #2)
IF SHE RAN (Book #3)
IF SHE HID (Book #4)
IF SHE FLED (Book #5)
IF SHE FEARED (Book #6)
IF SHE HEARD (Book #7)

THE MAKING OF RILEY PAIGE SERIES
WATCHING (Book #1)
WAITING (Book #2)
LURING (Book #3)
TAKING (Book #4)
STALKING (Book #5)

KILLING (Book #6)

RILEY PAIGE MYSTERY SERIES

ONCE GONE (Book #1)
ONCE TAKEN (Book #2)
ONCE CRAVED (Book #3)
ONCE LURED (Book #4)
ONCE HUNTED (Book #5)
ONCE PINED (Book #6)
ONCE FORSAKEN (Book #7)
ONCE COLD (Book #8)
ONCE STALKED (Book #9)
ONCE LOST (Book #10)
ONCE BURIED (Book #11)
ONCE BOUND (Book #12)
ONCE TRAPPED (Book #13)
ONCE DORMANT (Book #14)
ONCE SHUNNED (Book #15)
ONCE MISSED (Book #16)
ONCE CHOSEN (Book #17)

MACKENZIE WHITE MYSTERY SERIES

BEFORE HE KILLS (Book #1)
BEFORE HE SEES (Book #2)
BEFORE HE COVETS (Book #3)
BEFORE HE TAKES (Book #4)
BEFORE HE NEEDS (Book #5)
BEFORE HE FEELS (Book #6)
BEFORE HE SINS (Book #7)
BEFORE HE HUNTS (Book #8)
BEFORE HE PREYS (Book #9)
BEFORE HE LONGS (Book #10)
BEFORE HE LAPSES (Book #11)
BEFORE HE ENVIES (Book #12)
BEFORE HE STALKS (Book #13)
BEFORE HE HARMS (Book #14)

AVERY BLACK MYSTERY SERIES

CAUSE TO KILL (Book #1)

CAUSE TO RUN (Book #2)
CAUSE TO HIDE (Book #3)
CAUSE TO FEAR (Book #4)
CAUSE TO SAVE (Book #5)
CAUSE TO DREAD (Book #6)

KERI LOCKE MYSTERY SERIES
A TRACE OF DEATH (Book #1)
A TRACE OF MUDER (Book #2)
A TRACE OF VICE (Book #3)
A TRACE OF CRIME (Book #4)
A TRACE OF HOPE (Book #5)